# Highland
# Awakening

## By
## Kathryn Lynn Davis

Duncurra LLC

www.duncurra.com

Copyright 2015 by Kathryn Lynn Davis

ISBN-13: 978-1-942623-30-4

Cover Art by Earthly Charms

Produced in the USA

# Dedication

To my father, Mickey Davis, whose response to this story gave me lingering inspiration, I love you, Dad.

And to my dearest sister, now and always, Susan Cusack. You have helped me breathe no matter how deep the water got.

# Acknowledgements

First and foremost, I want to thank my husband Michael, whose patience seems to grow as I procrastinate more and more.

I also want to thank my Guardian sisters, especially Lily Baldwin and Sue-Ellen Welfonder, who helped me take this chance, as well as Ceci Giltenan, Victoria Zak, Tarah Scott, and Kate Robbins.

And to my blood sister Anne, who encourages me in any way she can, and lets me know she believes in me.

Finally, thank you Sharon Frizzell and Ashley Reader Granger for unwavering enthusiasm and support.

# Chapter 1

*Glen Affric, Scottish Highlands*
*1811*

The mist rose and fell like gauze before a windowpane, blocking Esmé's sight, and then revealing the late winter world to her in softly sharpened detail. She was crouched behind a half-buried boulder, shuddering with cold and apprehension as she peered through the yellow cotton grass beyond the boulder that hid her from her father. The huge bear rose on its hind legs, snarling when it sensed danger nearby. The mist hovered for a moment, highlighting its glistening white teeth—sharp and deadly—then dropped like a thick, wet curtain of white, blinding her. She had seen the marks of those teeth on the sheep the beast had mangled, whose carcasses it had left behind. She shivered, hands clasped tight, terrified.

Enveloped in the moisture that cut off both sight and sound, she remembered how, throughout the winter, this bear had terrorized the valley of Glen Affric and the manor house at the Hill of the Hounds where Esmé and her family lived. The huge animal had come out of hibernation too soon, and winter had hung on too long, and for reasons no one understood, it hovered around the crofts and manor at night, killing sheep and chickens and goats instead of moving south, where the air was warmer and prey was more plentiful.

The people of the Glen had been afraid to go out at night, and one man had been killed when he tried to hunt the beast down. Everyone was spooked by the creature, so Connall Fraser, Esmé's father, the owner of the Hill of the Hounds and keeper of his tenants, had a whispered conversation with Caelia Rose and Rory MacGregor, his in-laws. Esmé, who was not afraid of anything, crept out of bed—leaving her young brother Ewan snuggled among the covers. He often came to talk to her at night when bad dreams beset him, and usually ended up sleeping in her bed.

She had tiptoed up to the doorway in the sitting room to listen as her father, whom she thought very brave, declared that he would hunt down the Beast until he killed it, and his family and tenants and friends would be safe once again. He might as well have spoken the motto of the Fraser Clan: 'I am ready!'

He set off that very night, musket and knife in hand, so intent on his object, he was unaware that his nine-year-old daughter was following him, wrapped tight in her heavy wool cloak.

She, in turn, was not aware that she was followed.

Blond-haired Esmé was warm, but she shivered with excitement. "What a great adventure!" she whispered, adding the Fraser war cry with vehemence. "*Caisteal Dhuni!*" She ran lightly from birch to oak to alder to pine so Connall would not spot her. She breathed in the taste and smell of the grasses and trees and water all around her—those not still covered with snow or with ice hanging from the branches— her heart racing in anticipation.

Connall Fraser carried a small bladder, which he hoped would mask the smell of the meat until he was ready. He took out half a fist-sized morsels and moved deeper into the dark forest, placing them just above bear height so the animal would have to struggle to get to them. As he worked, the mist fell like insubstantial snow, playing tricks with the odor of the meat and calming the breeze until everything but Connall Fraser and his daughter were still.

The meat was bait; the height his chance to catch the giant unaware. Every few feet, he stopped to listen, absorbing every sound and odor and movement, until he knew exactly where he was, and where the night birds rested and the wildcats huddled in nest and cave. He sniffed the thick Highland air, chilled and heavy with mist, murmuring, "Not long now."

Staying far enough away that he would not see or hear her, Esmé copied his movements, thrilled by the hunt, by his ignorance of her presence, by the challenge they faced that night. She heard rustling near at hand and covered her mouth to stifle her involuntary cry, catching it just in time.

Her father knelt, raising the rifle, watching and waiting for just one glimpse of the Beast. He could feel it nearby; the hair on his neck stood on end and goose bumps rose along his arms. He steadied the rifle as the animal moved from tree to tree, seeking more of the meat left high in the branches.

Connall saw the creature's outline through the failing light of the crescent moon, aimed and released the trigger.

The bear roared in pain, stumbled, clung to the tree and righted himself. He wavered for a moment, growling and snarling as he tossed his head back and forth.

Behind her boulder, Esmé grabbed her hip and stifled several screams that rose in her throat. She could feel the burning, the rage, the pain beyond bearing just as if her father had shot her instead of the bear. Finally she could not hold it in any longer; she screamed in agony as she watched in slow-motion while her father prepared to fire again. He flinched, turned and saw her, and lost his grip on the rifle.

Abruptly, the bear stopped, motionless, sniffed, and began to stumble toward Connall, who grabbed wildly for his gun and dirk at the same time. Still reeling with agony, Esmé swayed as something struck her in the chest like a physical blow.

She had always felt an affinity with animals, but never like this. The bear met her eyes and his yellow eyes begged her just before he collided with her father and the mist fell, obscuring her view, slowing the rapid beat of her heat. A shot exploded from the rifle and her father cried out harshly, in panic.

"Da!" she screamed. "No!" Her father was inside her in his fear and rage and instinct. The bear was inside her in his torment. Each was part of her; she could not choose. "Da!" she screamed again and again, scrambling blindly through curtain after white, stifling curtain.

She became confused, turning in circles, until her father called for her shakily. "Esmé!"

Moving quickly through the undulating surface of the mist, she reached his side and collapsed there. Only then did it strike her that the bear's pain was gone. "Are ye hurt?" But she knew he was. "Where is he?" She glanced warily over her shoulder.

"Gone," Connall choked out. "I don't know why. He knocked the rifle out of my hand, clawing my arm, and I fell back on my knife, and while I lay there, he just—went away."

Busy examining his wounds, the girl opened and closed her mouth on sounds of horror that would not come. Esmé sat frozen in place. "Da," she whispered at last, "my Da..." *You have to do something,* she told herself without a sound. *But I'm only nine!* she replied desperately, in silence. *Old enough for it to be your fault!* She felt as if she were strangling, as if the knife had pierced her own shoulder.

"I'm sorry, Da!" she cried as her feet were released at last from the moist night soil and her hands from the rough boulder. With all her strength and fear and guilt, she touched Connall's shoulder gently. Using her teeth, she ripped strips from her petticoat, balled one up to press against the wound, and wound the others around his shoulder, tying them to keep the blood from flowing. Then she paused to catch her breath. She could not help but stare at the deep ugly marks from the claws. Again, she felt her father's pain, and her heart pounded, stealing her breath.

"I can help," she said between chattering teeth. Tearing off more cloth, she fashioned a rough sling, cupped his injured arm in it and tied it above his shoulder. "Forgive me, Da, I never meant—"

"I know." His voice became more hoarse by the minute.

Esmé knelt beside him in tears, her silver-grey eyes full of regret and dread. "I have to get ye home. Do ye think ye can stand?"

Connall cleared his throat painfully. *Doesn't matter what I think. I have to do this for my daughter. No choice.* Esmé stood as close as she could get and helped him up. She winced when he groaned more than once, but he finally stood upright. She draped his good arm around her slender shoulders.

"We'll get ye home and send for the healer. Come here." They limped back to the Hill slowly as the mist closed around them, holding each other as tight as they could, though it made their pain worse.

The girl slept in a chair beside her father while Eachan the healer worked, spreading on tincture of iodine to disinfect the wounds, giving a decoction of yew for the pain, making poultice after poultice of skunk cabbage and kelp to help draw the toxins from the wounds, and pennyroyal and yarrow root to break the fever. Connall moaned and twisted, unable to rest, so finally Eachan gave him an infusion of black willow and hops to sedate him. At last he fell into a restless sleep.

Esmé sat staring for hours, trying to understand what had happened. When she felt the bear's burning pain, it had shocked her. She didn't understand why the mist had kept falling just when she needed most to see. She had felt her father's pain as well, and that was something she could not endure. Her own was enough and more than enough. She knew—though she did not want to admit it—that some kind of power had taken her over tonight, and it left her frightened, bewildered and confused.

Her grandmother Caelia Rose MacGregor, sat beside her and took her hand. "Can I help ye, Esmé? Is there anything I can do?"

Esmé loved her grandmother more than just about anyone else. She understood so many things, and Esmé could tell her anything. But not this. She could never speak of this to anyone. Ever.

Not until the next morning when Esmé went up to her room, did she discover Ewan's night rail and a hat he always wore outdoors on her floor. She sensed at once that her little brother, aged six, must have followed her into the night. But he had not followed her home.

He had vanished.

# Chapter 2

*The Isle of Lewis*
*1820: eleven years later*

*Magnus MacLeod smiled in his sleep, which helped soften the usual scowl he displayed day and night of late. He felt light, as if he weighed nothing at all—a patent impossibility at 6'1", with muscles lean and hardened from the life that had been thrust upon him. Bouncing about in his dream as he used to do when a child, he ran and ran— wild and free and happy. Even in his sleep he growled a rebuttal, but he couldn't deny it was different in this pale green land, this yellow-blue-green fertile land.*

*He frowned, nose twitching when it came to him that though he was laughing and shouting like a child, he was just as tall and ungainly as ever. "Legs too long," he muttered incoherently. "Always have been." He stomped the undulating ground, one foot after the other, as if to shorten his lengthy calves and thighs, shaking his head at his own daft efforts. Except his legs got shorter. Gaping, astonished, he tried to back away from them. "None o' that funny stuff," he warned sternly, though who or what he was warning he could not guess, because no one else was there.*

*Magnus shuddered when he caught a whiff of charcoal breezing past. "Have to get out of here," he mumbled, even less comprehensibly than before. "Tis daft, daft, dangerous." But when he tried to scramble away from a giant tent that was colored so like the forest of rowan, oak and pine, that it had blended with the background, his feet did not move—or they moved a little, but he stumbled, because he wasn't used to his long torso on such runty legs.*

*All at once he was not certain it was actually him swaying back and forth so far each way he thought he*

7

*might be sick. His body was moving—or trying to—but his mind was oddly detached. He was torn, physique from concentration, yet enveloped by distant music—drumbeat and reed whistle—seductive and hypnotic, drawing him into the peculiar tent that stretched to the edge of his sight and beyond. Without being aware of it, he began to move— unsteadily, wary and perplexed. The music filled his head: not a song, but a thing whole in and of itself, like the wind or the cold winter rain. Gradually, glowing with a soft yellow light at first, a sound burst forth, incandescent, and resolved itself into a voice:* "Arise," *it sang in a tone like melted caramel,* "the whole of the world awaits me."*

He awoke suddenly—his long, lean body slick with sweat, arms and legs tingling—to realize that the dream, The Voice had indeed aroused him, creeping up along his neck, around his ears and along his shoulder blades. It clung to him, tracing the skin on his belly and tugging the dark hair that disappeared into the worn pair of breeches he slept in. He felt light-headed, as though he needed something. Something he had lost in the dream.

The awkwardly shaped stone room was unfamiliar for a long moment.

"No, ye blackguard!" he shouted to the voice or the chilled emptiness; he wasn't sure which. Anger raced like liquid fire through his veins, because he could not leave the remnants of that unsettling dream behind. He didn't like it: this disorientation. He liked—no needed—to know exactly where he was, exactly what was what.

Bed, rug, chest, stone ceiling, heavy purple velvet curtain. They looked vaguely like things he had owned once. A flicker of comfort cracked his chest. He was sure they were familiar. "Mine," he said with emphasis in case the empty room might argue. Safety was near; he could smell it, like heather in the dew-touched morning. He was grateful even for the thick rim of ice over the ewer holding his washing water, because he saw it every day. It was dependable, normal. Though the sky he could see through his high crescent window was still dark, he shattered the ice with his elbow and dumped the lot over his black hair and into the chipped basin, shuddering and snorting as he did so. He was not going to risk returning to bed.

"When will this cursed winter leave me in peace?" he bellowed. And realized he was free. The dream was gone.

But its loss meant the return of the tormenting memory of other things lost. He clenched his fists around the cracked basin, threatening to break it straight across. "Julia," he snarled at the water, as if he could see there her lovely, elegant face, surrounded by her upswept dark hair, braided like a crown. "You're no princess to me, ye—" he could not quite bring himself to call her a whore, though his betrothed had left him for another man—a bookkeeper from Edinburgh, no less! He and she had been betrothed since childhood: "to put an end to the feuds between the two clans," his parents had explained in tandem. Magnus was now laird of the MacLeods of Lewis, and Julia the daughter of the current laird of the MacDonnells of Glengarry. In Magnus's view, for 50 years past those feuds had become no more or less than nuisances that burst into flame at a few heated tempers, the flames dying out as quickly as they'd risen.

"Now you've given them a real reason for a feud, ye foolish girl." He still spoke into the water as if her image were there. *That's no' the real problem, and ye know it,* he told himself. *Tis that ye were falling in love with her.*

"I wasn't!" he declared belligerently. *Then what's that hole in your heart? And the grimace on your face, day after day?*

"I'm worried about this endless winter. About feeding our people. As a laird should be." *Hmmph! In love is what ye are.*

Magnus felt ridiculous when he realized he was speaking to a basin of water as if it were a woman long gone from his sight, and having a conversation with his thoughts. "What is *wrong* with me today?"

"Weel, I could tell ye that if ye give me an hour or two."

Magnus closed his eyes in an expression of long-suffering patience and pushed back all the things that rushed to his tongue in a desperate need to be spoken. "What is it, Graeme? I've told ye to leave me in peace down here." Surreptitiously he glanced at the velvet curtain and was relieved to see it was completely closed.

"We're waiting for ye at breakfast. Ye'd best hurry."

Pointing up at the window, Magnus grumbled, "Tis no' yet dawn." He was immediately suspicious. "Why would ye do that?" Despite his doubts, he hurried his brother out of the room and down the stairs toward where the dining room of Lewis Castle had been more or less restored.

"Da just wants the family to eat all together." Graeme rushed the words, pushing them together.

"In the middle of the night?" He knew better, but something in Graeme's demeanor set his teeth on edge. Muscles tense, Magnus stepped in front, blocking his brother's way. "Why?"

Graeme, both taller and broader than his older brother, seemed to shrink where he stood. "How would I know? He doesn't tell me his plans—just gives me orders."

Shaking his head in distrust, the laird turned and continued down the narrow, chipped stone stairs. He had suggested they abandon the castle for the ruin it was and build a manor house instead, but both brothers and his father had stood against him. *Tis just no' practical*, he'd explained. *It costs far too much and we're no' a wealthy clan.* He had argued for days and weeks and months, but they had won in the end.

He knew from the way Graeme was acting that they wanted something else today; they always ate breakfast without him. And most other meals as well. Preparing himself as if for war, he stepped over the last threshold and into the dining room.

~ * ~

"Magnus, lad, tis good to see ye this fine morning," his father, Diarmid MacLeod greeted his oldest son with gusto, though he usually could not be bothered to rouse himself when Magnus entered the room. The old laird had been a soldier in the Black Watch, where he'd received a wound in his leg that had festered while he was on campaign. It had not been treated properly, though Magnus, who was a healer, kept from pointing out with great difficulty when his father waxed on about the loyalty and splendor and unimpeachable perfection of everything about his former regiment, including the doctors.

"Tis drizzling, Da," his third son, Hugh reminded him. "Again." He watched a drop of water as it dripped from the arched ceiling, but did nothing to stop it from landing in the platter of trout.

"You're looking well this morning, Da. What gets ye out of bed so very long before dawn?" Magnus repeated his distaste for the early hour, perplexed. For years his father had been retreating: from society, from the outdoors, and from his duties. He had managed with his gamey leg until his wife died six years earlier, when he resigned his lairdship and turned it over to Magnus. His once handsome face was pale and wrinkled, his hair white and usually stringy. His shoulders slumped the more he disappeared into his study by the sea, where he charted the seabirds with strict attention. Until a few months ago he had stopped doing even that. He had once been a very different man: intelligent, forward thinking, affectionate, who had worked at bringing the MacLeods into the new and strange world Scotland had become. Magnus had admired that man and been been proud to follow him. But that man had given up when he lost his wife, and now he was slipping backward.

However, this morning Diarmid was standing straighter; his hair had been carefully combed; he wore a snowy white linen shirt and satin breeches, all of which perplexed Magnus mightily, though he was delighted by the change.

His brothers Hugh and Graeme stood on either side of their father, both brown-haired, Graeme more or less handsome, and Hugh rugged-looking. They were both taller than Magnus, soldiers, whose muscular bodies filled out a uniform nicely, as his young cousin Mairi had once told him.

The three of them, arrayed across the table from him as they were, did not frighten him, though he did not have their physical might. Instead he had the tiniest impulse to laugh, but he kept it in check. "Yes?" he said politely, inclining his head ever so slightly.

"Now see here!" His father leaned over, pounding the table with his clenched fist. He winced visibly, which detracted from the drama somewhat. "We're tired of waiting for you to do what you aught! The MacDonnell wench has humiliated you publically, and therefore all of Clan MacLeod. Tis no' to be borne, do ye hear! Ye must take the role of laird and behave accordingly, or I'll…" He sagged a bit and began to cough. "I swear I'll—" He slumped down to the chair suddenly, coughing and choking, holding his throat and gasping.

Magnus leapt over three chairs and reached the sideboard in seconds. He retrieved a bottle of pale purplish liquid and a spoon on his way back across the chairs. Deciding over the table was the quickest way to advance, he put one foot on a chair and lifted himself over, landing quietly beside his father.

"Da," he said gently, "listen to me. Let me help ye sit up straight." The man still had incredible strength for as sunken and defeated as he looked some days. It took everything Magnus had to get him to stop wrenching his body back and forth without hurting himself. "That's it. No, I'm here, ye won't fall. Now try to breathe in and out while I get ye a spoonful of my special tisane."

The coughing slowed somewhat but it still sounded hollow and raw. While his brothers stared blankly, Magnus managed to get the tisane down Diarmid's throat.

"Now lean back and relax, Da. No, ye won't fall. I've got ye. You're all right now. Does your throat feel better?"

The sound of his musical voice did much to calm troubled waters. Until Hugh pushed ahead of Graeme. "We've decided, the three of us, that ye must go take the men and lead them on a raid straight to The MacDonnells of Glengarry's front door. Make him hurt for what he's done to us. Make him force his daughter to honor the betrothal."

"Else there'll be war between the two clans," Graeme finished for him.

Magnus gaped at them, waiting for them to laugh at the joke, but they did not. He was silent for the longest time while their 'suggestions' clattered around in his head. "Ye don't start a war over a broken betrothal anymore," he pointed out at last. Though he had yearned for Julia a short time past, the thought of attacking the MacDonnell stronghold, and then having her father drag her back here, forcing her to marry Magnus—it made him feel slightly bilious. He simply did not want a woman who did not want him, and if his knot-headed brothers couldn't see that...

"Our pride is at stake!" Graeme bellowed far too loudly. "You're making us look a cesspool of fools."

*Cesspool of fools,* Magnus thought. *Precisely.*

"Tell him what you're going to do if he doesn't restore our pride!" Hugh poked his father in the shoulder. "Tell him!"

Diarmid MacLeod looked up at the son who had leapt to his aid when he began to cough, at the son who had kept him from curling in upon himself, which would have made him choke to death, no doubt. The son who, even now, was holding him upright, just to be sure.

"Tell him what you'll do with the title of laird," Graeme insisted.

"I'll take it away," their da croaked through an irritated throat, "and give it to Graeme if ye don't give a care for our honor, Magnus, for it doesn't seem to me that ye do.

# Chapter 3

*Glen Affric*

*The first time she dreamed, Esmé felt only joy and jubilation slipping through her blood, almost—but not quite—singing. The rhythm of rejoicing filled her in a way she'd never felt before, as if she were discovering something altogether new and irresistible. The rhythm became a soft echo of drums in the distance, calling her, as did the grass and flowers, which grew so vibrant and intense they lifted her from the ferny bed in which she lay.*

*But no, that wasn't right. She was in her own bed at home, where the leaves did not burst like stars, so full of happiness were they. The drums and a harp and, quietly, quietly, the flitter, flirt of a reed whistle calling. The colors were so pure, the music so alluring that the blossoms kissed her hands and the notes raised chills along her arms.*

*She was lost to all that was familiar, all that was comfortable, and yet she had never felt safer—or more passionate. And then she heard the thin thread of a voice rise from the harp strings, and all at once it was inside her, and the song was her song, and the beauty her beauty. She longed to stretch out in the small pool under the shady oaks, to bury her feet in the soft, silken silt, and let her long blonde hair flow out behind her. Without a word, the voice inside her told her she could not reach so far. Not yet.*

*Whose voice was it? Who was whispering to her? She tried to reach out, just a little, because she had been her own prisoner for so long, but found her body curled in on itself, as it did when she was lonely or afraid. Or when she thought of Ewan. Except now she was enveloped in a veil so fine, so gauzy it might shatter with a breath, yet she knew it was her shield, her armor. And she felt at ease, at peace, as if the whole of the world that daily threatened her, had turned into this place flowing with life and color and song. It was a celebration, and even her doubts could not dim her joy, because it was not of her mind, but of her senses. She reveled in those senses, light as a soap bubble, floating on air.*

And when the music faded into the faint echo of harp strings and a distant recorder in the quivering grasses touched by the rising sun, she tried to open her eyes, but it was too difficult. She blinked and blinked again, trying to dissolve the veil that left everything blurred and indistinct, as if it were the first time she had ever opened her eyes and tried to see. When at last the veil fell away, everything glimmered and shone with new, vivid intensity. Esmé gave a little gasp and leaned forward on her mattress, entranced by the vibrant hues. The song came back to her as she crouched, smiling: a reed whistle and hand harp mingling in a soft, seductive tune. For an instant the dream was alive again.

She felt a disconcerting warmth in the pocket of her night rail. Carefully she removed what lay inside, closing her fist tightly around it. Gradually, lips parted in anticipation, she opened her fingers one-by-one to reveal the gold medallion in her palm. She had found it years ago while planting herbs in her special garden, and she knew it was very old. She'd looked among her grandfather's books in the crowded library at the Hill of the Hounds, discovered the pattern had come from the time before the Romans. She treasured it above all things and was amazed that the dream had affected it so. It glowed, warm and beautiful in her palm. She pressed it to her cheek and the warmth passed through her body like the steady burn of a firefly in her blood. Smiling, she slipped it back into her pocket. Somehow The Voice had touched her deeply, in a way she would never forget.

~ * ~

Dressing quickly in trews made of the red Rose plaid and the plain muslin shirt she always wore when she worked in her garden, Esmé hurried downstairs. She had ruined more than one dress when she was younger, until her Grandmother, Caelia Rose MacGregor, began to make her these boy's clothes, so she would not drag more dresses in the loam. Esmé was clever with a needle, and was soon making her own clothes, and her sister's, much to Caelia's relief. The girl was happy that her grandmother now had time to get back to her painting with pastels. There was some MacGregor plaid around the house, but mostly it was the Rose.

"Why, Grandda?" Esmé asked Rory MacGregor once.

Brow furrowed over his hazel eyes, he thought for a moment. "'Tis because my family was lost to me long ago, and the Roses took me in and made me one of their own."

"But how were they lost to ye?" she persisted, as only a young child will.

"'Tis a long, complicated story, lass, and I'll tell ye one day when you're older."

Nodding solemnly, Esmé jumped down from his lap, stopping for a moment to say, "I'm glad ye came to us, Grandda." She scampered away before he could reply.

Now, on the morning of the dream, with its magic lingering about her shoulders, Esmé crept downstairs and along the hall to the door just beside the kitchen. As always, she paused with her hand on the doorknob, heart racing. Her palms grew damp with sweat as she slid back the bolt and tried to turn the knob. It slipped through her hands once, twice. She dried her palms on her trews and made one more attempt; this time it turned and she pulled the door open slowly, until she stood with both feet on the threshold. Swallowing dryly, she looked around at the cozy garden full of herbs and late winter flowers and crates for injured animals, sniffing the scent of pines that wafted over the tall stone walls. As always, she had to remind herself of the beauty in this place, the safety, before she could take a single step outside. *Tis your haven, Esmé, don't be an eejit.*

With that she moved into the garden, closing the door behind her so she could not turn back. Other than to work in this private little garden, she not set foot outside the house at Hill of the Hounds since she was nine and the tragedy happened. *Bad things happen when I go outside*, she told her family when they asked her why. She had hated feeling the bear's pain, the agony she'd caused her father; she'd hated her ignorance about Ewan. She should have looked for him as soon as they got home. And oh, how her father and his only son had suffered. Ewan had been horribly ill for several weeks, and then he died. *My fault. All mine!* She would never take that risk again.

Brushing the dark thoughts aside, she went to her menagerie and took a jack-rabbit out that had injured its foot. She calmed it by looking it straight in the eye and humming a tune. Slowly, it relaxed, lay its head between its front paws and closed its eyes.

Esmé continued to hum an ancient tune, gift of the Old Ones, as she clipped off the bandage and examined the stitches on the back paw. The wound was healing nicely, and she could feel there was no poison flowing through the rabbit's blood. Its heartbeat was steady and pure, its pulse untainted by infection. She lay her cheek against its flank and smiled. Deftly, before it woke from its daze, she snipped the stitches with her embroidery scissors, put on one more application of garlic and set the animal down.

She could have sworn by the Tuatha de Dannan—the ancient Celtic Gods—that the animal smiled at her. So she smiled back.

Most lowlanders worshipped the new and were slowly forgetting the old, as were the Highlanders, who had once held fast to the legends and traditions of the past, believing, as Esmé and Caelia and Rory did, that these thing were the heart and soul of Scotland—what made it great and rooted so deeply in the soul.

Esmé looked around at her garden of starflowers and daisies struggling through the chilly soil, though it was nearly June. The winter simply would not let go. Still, the branches of rose bushes spread and tangled their way up the uneven stone walls with tiny pink and red buds that fell off the vine before they bloomed. Moss and ferns grew along both sides of the tiny burn her grandfather Rory had dug for her, then guided the large burn outside to split off and supply her garden with peat-brown water running over stones. In spite of herself, Breda the brat came out, crouching for hours beside the stream, placing rocks of various sizes to create a pond and a tiny waterfall, a burn that rippled over smooth, round stones.

This small walled garden was the only place where Esmé ventured to visit the outdoors, because she was safe here; here she had control, though she never forgot her fear and guilt. They all had lost so much that night. That's why she had studied with Eachan, the healer who had saved her father, learning all she could about herbs and poultices and teas. She never wanted to feel so helpless a second time.

"Ye have that look on your face again," her father said, coming up behind her.

Startled but not distressed, she crossed her legs and sat on the ground that she kept soft, by turning it over and over, despite the chilly weather. Outside her enclosure there was snow and frigid wind, but not inside. She and Connall Fraser had made sure of that. "Ye shouldn't creep up on me, Da. Ye know how fragile I am." For once, her tone was light-hearted.

"Oh, aye?" Connall shook his head, though she *was* fragile in some ways; in others, she was incredibly strong. He wished, as he had so often, that he understood her better. "I'll try to stomp louder from now on." He pointed to the rabbit. "Have ye been doing your healing again?" He barely kept himself from emphasizing 'healing' with a tiny bit of sarcasm. Her healing frightened him sometimes, so he often responded with skepticism or anger.

"Aye, he's free of infection; I felt it."

Connall Fraser stiffened as anger flashed, stifling the fear. "Ye can hear things in the beat of his heart, no doubt, but I doubt ye can 'feel' what he feels. Tis just no' the same, Esmé, lass."

Sighing, she put the rabbit in the clever cage her father had built, which gave him air and light and even grass, but kept him safe from the other animals. "I forgot we can no' discuss such things, Da. We agreed, did we no'? Ye believe what gives ye comfort and I'll do the same." Her hazel eyes, more silver than grey, begged him to leave it at that.

"So we did, and so we shall." He glanced around at the tall walls he had built for her, with occasional windows to let in more light. They had worked together on designing the cages, with Grandfather Rory suggesting a few clever touches. Grandmother Caelia had helped the girl lay out and plant the herbs she needed for her healing, and even the reluctant Breda had helped—in her own way.

Connall felt he owed this sanctuary to his daughter, because of the guilt she carried on her slender shoulders. He would rather have removed that guilt entirely, but he did not begin to know how. So he did what he could for Esmé, his multi-talented, sensitive daughter. She made him ache sometimes, such as now, simply by smiling.

"Thank ye, Da."

He was not certain to what she was referring, but her gratitude warmed his heart regardless. "I came out to tell ye your grandmother is bringing ye some food, since ye missed breakfast with us. Are ye well, my lassie?"

Esmé hesitated. "I'm well," she said, though she was not certain that was true. "Tis just a dream I had."

Her father clenched his fists. "A nightmare? Are they

back?"

Throwing her arms around him, Esmé cried, "No, Da! Tis nothing like that. Don't worry about me so much. *It was magic,* she wanted to cry; *I feel it in every bone in my body. But good magic or bad?* Her blood sang, *ye know tis good. Tis frightening. Tis beautiful!* But she did not say those things. They were her secret.

"Ah, here Caelia is now with Geordie trailing behind her."

Geordie was the youngest Fraser child. The result of a brief blissful year when Sorcha Fraser had stayed home for a while, temporarily happy in the bosom of her family. She had gone soon enough when the hard work of raising a screaming baby began, though strangely, after she left, Geordie became a laughing, playful infant very quickly.

Connall Fraser—the only man brave enough to marry Esmé's mother—was handsome. He would have had to be, to catch Sorcha MacGregor and make her fall in love with him. But he'd made a mistake; he wanted a family and a secure life. He wanted to know what was going to happen tomorrow.

Esmé and Breda's mother had never really wanted a family. Instead, Caelia and Rory's only daughter had roamed the world, going from man to man after she left Connall. Esmé was grateful every day that Sorcha'd had the good sense to leave her family at the Hill of the Hounds. It had saved them all.

Connall kissed his daughter on the forehead, nodded to his mother-in-law and started back inside.

He was nearly knocked off his feet by little Geordie hurling himself at Esmé and grabbing her around the knees. "I missed you, Esmé. You weren't at breakfast."

The girl laughed and swung him around in her arms. "I missed ye too, laddie. But everyone else was there, surely." She tousled his tawny hair.

"Aye, but the grown-ups were all busy, and Breda was

frowning. Besides, she's never as funny as ye."

Their father's lips twitched while he tried to swallow his laughter. Connall lifted his son and kissed the top of his head. "Just don't tell Breda ye said that, lad. She'd choke on it for certain.

In the act of hugging his father, Geordie paused, looking confused. "Tis only words, Da. How could she choke? I didn't mean to kill her. I'll never say it again."

For a second time, Connall's lips twitched, along with Esmé's and Grandmam Caelia's. "That would probably be wise," Caelia said quite seriously, in order to keep her laughter inside.

"Weel, I've work to do," Connall said, hurrying away, shoulders shaking.

"Be a good lad, *mo-run*, and go play with your garden toys while I sit and talk with your sister."

Geordie nodded good-naturedly, gave Esmé one more ferocious hug and went off to dig out his 'tools' and wooden worms, carved and lacquered birds and small animals his Grandad Rory had carved for him to play with while he pretended to plant a garden like Esmé's. He adored Esmé and wanted to be exactly like her. He knew with certainty that she would never leave him.

"I brought ye something in case you're hungry." Caelia Rose MacGregor sat on the edge of the chair her son-in-law had built for her comfort when she visited Esmé in the garden, which was often.

"Thank ye, Grandmam. I guess I'm just no' hungry."

Caelia balanced a tray of bannocks and crowdie and pears on one wide, flat arm of the chair. Normally the girl would have at least stopped by the kitchen long enough to bring her food out to share among her menagerie of animals on the mend, those who'd chosen to stay after they'd healed, and some who came and went when they pleased. This late May day was cold, so the garden was more crowded than usual, and the pens and ingenious boxes where she kept the injured and sick were full to bursting.

Examining Esmé closely, Caelia observed, "Ye have a distant look in your eyes, Esmé Rose, as if you're no' quite with us."

Rose was her middle name, but also Caelia's maiden name. The girl loved the sound of her two names together, and clung to all things Rose. She loved the crest, which had a harp—an old-fashioned hand harp, or *clarsach*—instead of the animals of prey others had chosen long ago. Besides, music enchanted her, so it was perfect. Birds stood on either side of the *clarsach*, as opposed to the bucks or wolves that appeared on other crests. And the Rose motto warmed her heart: Constant and True.

Inexplicably, the girl blushed and looked away. The added color in her cheeks emphasized her comeliness, but also her fragility. She was tall, yet delicate looking in every other sense, but her grandmother was not fooled by Esmé's looks. Caelia knew her to be a very strong woman for her 18 years. Her tightly braided blonde hair was pulled back from her heart-shaped face and fell down her back, brushing the soil. Caelia had long ago given up trying to keep her favorite granddaughter clean. Sometimes she wondered if the dirt was a form of unconscious protection.

"You've been dreaming again, haven't ye?"

Unable to control herself, the girl blushed a second time. "Have ye been talking to Da?"

"About your dreams? Certainly not. That subject will always remain between us. Ye must trust me on that, dear lass."

"I do." Esmé looked up when she felt the blush fade, though she knew Caelia had seen it. Her grandmother missed nothing. Sometimes she wondered if Caelia could read her mind. She certainly hoped not. The sensuous feelings came rushing back, and she dug her nails into the soil, hoping the memories would go underground, though her whole body trembled. Her grandmother was a seer, and though she told the girl time and again she could only 'see' through her paintings, Esmé was fanciful and could not help but wonder. "But I promise ye, these were new dreams not old nightmares. New visions and songs. New..." she hesitated, touching the medallion in her pocket, then added, "promises."

Caelia felt a special ache in her heart for this young woman, who had gone through so much when she was only nine, and without a mother to help her through it.

Esmé could not hold back a poignant smile. She knew her grandmother was thinking of The Night of the Bear as they all referred to it, because it had changed so much. Everyone had suffered many hard weeks after Esmé and her father had stumbled in the night of the attack. The healer Eachan had come quickly with his herbs and poultices. Still, her da had burned with fever for a full week, and then been ill for two more. It had taken him even longer to strengthen his arm again, for some of the muscles had been damaged. He had managed many of the required duties as Keeper of the Manor, and Rory helped him with others, but it had been well over a year before Esmé heard Connall confess to his in-laws: "I finally feel like a man again."

*I and I alone took that feeling from him,* she berated herself.

Meanwhile the men of Glen Affric had set out to search for Ewan, who had gotten lost in the woods when he followed Esmé. He had become very ill with a raging fever and congestion of the lungs, and though Eachan had treated him as vigilantly as her father, her young brother had only lasted a month. Too weak to fight anymore, he had finally given in. Esmé had been inconsolable. *I did this too! I should have taken care of my brother. I knew how he depended on me. For excitement, for a reckless moment, I brought disaster upon everyone.*

Weighed down with guilt and fear of losing more of

the ones she loved, she had huddled inside the manor house at Hill of the Hounds—or Fairies Haven, as some still called it—never once setting foot outside from that night forward, except for this small fenced area along the western side of the house. She had managed, over these many years, to push her guilt down deep inside, because it would have consumed her else.

They never discovered the injured bear.

For years she had been plagued by nightmares, and then dreamless sleep.

"Promises, is it?" her grandmother asked, pleased, for she could not resist Esmé's radiant face and smile. Her chest tightened with tenderness and tears pricked her eyes at the sight of her granddaughter's elation. "Weel then, tis time and not before time."

Esmé did not need to speak; the answer was in her shining eyes.

# Chapter 4

Magnus glowered at his brothers and father, holding steady, though it felt as if the ground was shifting like sand beneath his feet. Much as they often annoyed him, they were the only family he had left, and he cared for them profoundly.

He stared at them then as if he did not know them, had never known the two tall soldiers and the proud man, grizzled and weak, whose eyes flashed with resolve.

"Ye'd take away the lairdship?" he repeated in shock, feeling ill.

Diarmid nodded without a word.

"Ye are aware that I never wanted the title to begin with?" That was true; he'd had to fight a battle in his soul to even accept it, which was why he was stunned at how much this little plot to remove him from his birthright hurt.

Graeme sniggered. "Tis what ye say now to save yourself embarrassment, but we all know how much ye covet being laird for the power it gives ye over us, the clan and the money. Weel, now ye must pay for that power with a war."

His brown eyes seemed to pierce Magnus's defensive wall, and he realized his brother was smarter than he'd believed. Clever and greedy—for blood and violence, not money—that was a dangerous combination.

Pounding on the table with such force it rattled the plates and saucers, Hugh demanded, "Give us your answer. Is it to be war or no?"

His voice reverberated through the large room that should have held linen cabinets and several fine sideboards to display the china and silver and special pieces his family had cherished for generations. The table should have been of fine mahogany, and 20 feet long at least, with gilt cushioned chairs arranged along each side. Massive rugs should lie at both ends, woven in Brussels or the Far East, and the plain stone walls, cracked in some places, should have been covered with skilled and vibrant tapestries to give the huge room life and color. But as Magnus looked around at the new wooden floor—plain because that was all the MacLeods could afford—the six-foot oak table and newly upholstered eight matching chairs, he saw the dining room as a stranger would: bare and hollow and ludicrously empty.

The illness in his gut increased, and as it did, he knew what he must do. "I must consider it carefully." He looked directly at his father. "One cannot, after all, decide to go to war in the time it takes to miss breakfast. Julia MacDonnell has certainly destroyed her own honor, and that of her father, and laid a shadow across ours. You're right, the three of you. It cannot be allowed to stand."

That was not what they had expected. *Did they think I would capitulate while I stood with my stomach growling even through my shock and anger?* Of course they did. They not only had no faith in his judgment; they also had no faith in his strength, because he didn't wear it in a scabbard perpetually at his side. "But soon they'll find out how wrong they are," he said in a tone of voice neither his brothers nor his father would have recognized. He was fairly certain they had forgotten the subtlety of the MacLeod clan motto: "I shine, not burn." If, that is, they had ever understood it. He was certain Julia, his betrothed did not; she had not even bothered to learn it.

~ * ~

Magnus stopped briefly in his room to eat some cheese, bread and wine he'd had not had time to finish the night before. When it was gone, he was itching to get out and away from the castle. The sun had barely risen, but he knew others would be up and about. He reached the stairs from the Auld Keep to the town with great relief, more blind than open-eyed, thinking far too hard. He paused for a moment at the landing. Glancing down, he froze.

*Arise! The whole of the world awaits ye!* The Voice had said. And so it did.

The townspeople and half the island dwellers were gathered in one great jagged clump of humanity at the foot of the stairs and along the castle walls, all staring up at him expectantly. It was the end of May, but most of them stood in snow up to mid-calf, and the stones they were leaning on must be nearly as cold as the broken ice from the puddles in the muddy road. Winter lingered in patches on the thatched and wooden roofs, covering the ground beyond the crumbling city walls, half of which had collapsed years ago. The sea brushed the rocky shore lethargically, too thick and cold to rush. Water drip, drip, dripped from the corners of cottages, wooden shacks and a few newer buildings. It was 1820 on that day in late May, and the last hotel had been raised in 1750; the last bank in 1755. The keep behind him—called the Auld Keep, perhaps because it had been built in 1126—had fallen into to total disrepair in parts, but Magnus was only slowly bringing it back.

He enjoyed his other passions much more: he was the island healer, a benefactor to the people of his clan, and a scientist of sorts. At least he liked to think so. He was also a hunter and expert fisherman. He had tried to find ways to increase grain growth so the people didn't starve.

Magnus narrowed his bright blue eyes, running his fingers absently through his hair, waiting. *I've no' had my breakfast yet, so no doubt they want something done at once,* he thought cynically. He was not always so cynical, he told himself. Or was he?

"You're needed, Magnus the Broken!" several people cried out, both men and women.

He had once smashed two of his toes, and it irked him

that everyone since had called him Magnus the Broken. It might not have come to that if there hadn't been two other Magnuses in town. One was an old man who had been very ill, but against everyone's expectations, had survived. He was known as Magnus the Cured. The third was called just plain Magnus. "And a lucky man he is," Magnus the Broken murmured under his breath.

"What is the meaning of this?" he hollered down to the faces turned toward him. He did not really intend to be rude; it was just one of the hazards of being a MacLeod—but especially of being a Magnus. Besides, they all knew his gruff exterior was not the real Magnus; that was the Magnus he reserved for his family. And sometimes, of late, for memories of Julia MacDonnell. Particularly since Julia had left him—he cut the thought off ruthlessly. *I will not think about her. I have work to do.*

"Caitlin's boy's gone and broke his leg."

"You don't know it's broke, ye auld drunkard."

"Say that again and I'll lay ye flat," the first replied.

Magnus shouted an urgent plea, but it was too late. Soon fists were flying and petticoats ripping as the women used their sharp-toed boots to join in the fray.

Much as it had disturbed him, he considered slipping back into his dream. Instead, he hurried through the one remaining tower, found the narrow tunnel and scurried out the back way. Let them fight, perhaps use up some of their frustration with the winter that would not leave them. A good brawl always lifted their spirits.

Magnus himself was on his way to Caitlin and her son, Leith.

He wondered, not for the first time, why they did not call him Magnus the Healer. He had broken a head or five when they'd tried out that appellation, but that had never made a difference before. These seamen and farmers on the Isle of Lewis always did as they wished, regardless. Hardheaded Scottish lads and lasses, one and all.

In spite of himself, he grinned.

"Magnus!" A deep voice shouted from above. He recognized his next eldest brother, Graeme. Magnus ignored the sound as he would the creak of bent old metal. Both presaged trouble, and he already had an abundance of that.

"Magnus the Broken! If you're finally going to attack our deadliest enemy, MacDonnell of Glengarry, who promised ye a wife but graciously agreed she might break the betrothal with you when she met a handsome Findlay—if that's where you're headed with the riffraff on Lewis, ye might want to put on yer brogues and shield, and at least take a musket, if you've nothing better."

People began laughing in front and behind him, and all along the waterfront as well. "Bloody hell, ye bastard!" Magnus hissed under his breath. Graeme knew quite well he had nothing better, because Hugh had stolen the sword of the MacLeod of Lewis from the crumbling ruins of the Great Hall a week since. Though that room would take the most work, Magnus preferred keeping the ceremonial seal and family colors and the war swords on display there, as a reminder of the might they had once wielded.

He strongly suspected—no he knew outright—they would never wield it again, but he was not of a mind to care very much. Mostly he cared about the good health and security of the MacLeods, while his brothers, impractical fools that they were, dreamed of past glory and powerful warriors, and damsels in distress. They did not actually have to be in distress, so long as they viewed Graeme or Hugh as the rescuer in some small way.

His brothers were a never-ending trial to him, as was the castle, as was the title of Laird of Clan MacLeod of Lewis. He would love to leave the whole writhing mess of it in his brothers' laps and see what further chaos they would make of it. But now that they had challenged him, now that his father had threatened to take that title away—

he could not, would not give in.

Magnus smiled to himself. Graeme and Hugh thought they were frustrated with him. They had no idea what irritated was. But they were going to find out. He would personally make sure of it.

Meanwhile, Caitlin's Leith's leg needed attending to.

He arrived in her rickety building to notice snow still dripping through a hole in the roof and Leith lying on the worn settee, so tall he was hanging off both ends, though he was only 10. Magnus said a brief prayer for the widow Caitlin.

She came forward, flapping her apron in gratitude and apology. "Thank ye for comin', Laird. I'm sorry ye had to take the time."

Leith looked pale and listless—not like himself at all—but first things first. Magnus had to duck as he moved about the room; he had already struck his hard head twice, which resulted in more flapping, gratitude and apologizes. He resolved to move more carefully.

"Don't be sorry, Cait. Tis both my job and my calling. Could ye put some water in the heavy crock hanging above the fire?"

The spitting embers were set a little way back from the room in a narrow fireplace of plain curved stone; the chimney used to stand straight, but now tilted alarmingly because the rocks had shifted over the years. The stone walls were covered with thick mud to keep the cold out, and painted white give the room a sense of light. The windows with their shutters and leather curtains were tiny and did not give in much light. Still, Magnus thought, it was as cozy as it could be, with smell of peat mingling with the flow of the tangy sea air.

"Tis already near a boil," the housewife assured him. "Now come and see Leith. He's waiting for ye."

The boy's gloomy expression lightened as soon as he saw Magnus. "You'll fix everything, aye?" he asked, but it was not really a question. His eyes were full to the brim of confidence and hope.

"I'll do my best, lad." Magnus's voice was gravelly and he bent his head, digging into his bag of herbs and bottles and carefully separated leaves. He became preoccupied while spreading the wound with basil salve, despite his awkward fingers. "It doesn't matter if it goes beyond the edges," he explained to Leith and Caitlin. "The more medicine it spreads to keep away infection, the better. It will also keep the swelling down."

Mother and son nodded solemnly. Settling Caitlin in a chair with a mug of tea, the laird returned to see to Leith. "So, my lad, I hear ye had a struggle with a pylon.

The boy smiled weakly. "I want ye to know I won."

"I'd expect no less." Magnus answered without thinking; he was busy examining the lad's leg. He determined, by Leith's yelps of pain, that the bone in the front of his calf was broken.

He'd already asked several MacLeods to bring in snow packed down to ice in some kind of cloth they could tie around Leith's leg. It was swollen and purple, and he had to get that swelling down in order to set the broken bone. Magnus was happy to see how many were involved in the process of switching the cloths as the ice melted and replacing them with new. The men and women on the Isle of Lewis did not like to see their widows and children suffer.

Sitting with his back against the settee, Magnus nodded at them one-by-one.

"Tis, indeed a broken bone," he said softly. In an instant half a dozen townsmen rose to collect what he needed: two long narrow boards, many more or less clean rags to hold them in place. He waited to numb the deep slice on the boy's knee but he couldn't do the stitches alone.

"Can someone find young Sam for me?" he added.

"Leith needs her skill here today." A woman close to the door scurried off to seek out the small girl who resembled a street thug without the requisite size or muscles.

Magnus simply could not manipulate needle and thread through injured skin; his hands had always been too big. *He had always been too big, though not as large as his brothers.* But as muscular soldiers, women and men both admired Graeme and Hugh's size, because it represented strength of body and purpose. In sharp contrast, Magnus's hands were too large, the fingers too clumsy to perform many of the tasks a healer and a hunter and a scientist had to execute.

Sighing in frustration, he folded in upon himself—but it did not help. Thank God he had found Sam. He'd been able to save her from rats and starvation, and the bullies who lived hidden in the rocks and in the alleys between the facades of shops that had never quite been finished. He had fed her and given her clothes, which she hoarded rather than wearing, until the ones on her back fell apart at the seams. She had returned his favor to her a hundredfold. Magnus had taught her how to assist when more than one person was needed, how to prepare the simplest herbs, how to sew the critical stitches that held the edges of a wound together so it could heal properly.

He could always find her when he needed her, and vice versa. It was altogether a comfortable relationship. When she finally appeared in the doorway, looking as if she'd been adrift on a mud-spotted windy sea, Magnus could not help but smile. She wore a man's shirt, buttoned from top to bottom and tucked in thoroughly, but the sleeves hung down well past her wrists. Her breeks were torn at both knees and fit her badly, making her appear round where she was not and much more slender than she was. Her hair, dark-auburn-brown, stuck out round her head in a prickly halo, with half hanging loose, and half still contained in a careless braid.

Blinking once, Magnus got on his knees and bowed her in. "Join us, won't ye? I'm in need of your expertise."

Sam had been hoping for a more dramatic reaction, but she could never tell with the laird. Shrugging, she followed the path the townspeople cleared for her.

"First ye go back outside and wash in the trough, and ask Caitlin for a special clean bucket for your head," he whispered so no one else could hear. "Ye might even comb your hair. Then return to me, lass, for I could really use your help stitching this lad's wound and setting his leg.

Sam wanted to snap that she was fine as she was, but she knew it was a lie. She'd only come like this to test him. Once she saw how he bent his head so his hair fell forward over his face, but not in time to hide his quickly suppressed smile, she turned and was once again swallowed by the crowd.

Returning swiftly, hair combed, sleeves considerably less muddy and pushed high up on her arms, face and hands washed, she knelt on the other side of Leith and took the clean needle and unique thread Magnus handed her. The laird grinned at her transformation, nodding in approval.

Magnus had already given the lad a tincture of black willow and hops to sedate him, and decoction of yew for pain. Sam pursed her lips in concentration and began to sew, while Magnus did what he could to hold the sides of the wound together. Even with her small hands, the stitches were larger than they should be; she was always a bit nervous, and her fingers shook, though rarely did she lose control of the needle.

Leith held still, so as not to dislodge the ice packed around his leg. He kept his face expressionless while Caitlin held his shoulders, massaging his neck and looking away from the wound.

Magnus cursed inwardly, wishing he could do this more painlessly and effectively, but he did not yet know how. Still, he was learning, experimenting, teaching himself new things. At least the bullies left Samantha alone because she was his assistant. He wished he could do more for her too.

Once she was finished, Magnus examined the swelling in Leith's leg. It had gone down enough, and even if it had not, he did not want the boy to suffer anymore while he waited for the worst part.

Caitlin and Sam sat on his chest while two men held his leg and Magnus worked at fitting the broken ends of bone together. The young lad moaned and cried out, but the three men hastily put the narrow boards for the splint on either side and tied them firmly into place.

Forehead covered in sweat, Leith turned pale and fell unconscious against the arm of the settee.

"Let him rest," the laird told Caitlin. "He's had to face enough this day."

"As have ye, from the look of ye," Sam remarked outside the house.

"Och, ye need no' worry about me." Magnus was often surprised by her perception. This time it made him uneasy. He could not let the turbulence between him and his family show. He was strong enough to handle it alone. Or so he thought. "I'm weary is all."

Looking skeptical, Sam nevertheless held her tongue—for the time being.

~ * ~

Magnus managed to avoid Graeme and Hugh for the rest of the day. Come nightfall, he glanced outside his room to make sure no one was near, made a final check of the room itself, and satisfied himself that he was unobserved. He slipped behind the purple velvet curtain at the far side of the room, making certain it was closed behind him, before he turned up the oil lamp in the narrow stone room beyond. It opened into a corridor only he knew about, because he had gone through the ruins bit by bit after the family decided to restore them.

He had chosen this room specifically for this hidden corridor, where he had built long tables with small rings of stone for heating, drying stands, shelves full of bottles and various containers in strange shapes.

Magnus released his breath in relief. He felt at home here where he did his real work at night, partly because he did not wish to be disturbed, partly because he did not think others would understand what he was doing.

He took his avocation as a healer very seriously, and was always trying new herbs, new combinations, and using different parts of the herbs and wildflowers he'd asked Sam to gather last spring and summer, and even into the fall. He'd dried some, boiled some down, kept some moist, and practiced preserving some in the various receptacles he kept in his private room. He was often in there, curtain closed behind him, torches burning in the plain sconces on the battered stone walls. He tested and tasted, brewed and made poultices, teas and tisanes as he tried to extend his knowledge.

He had bought many books on the subject when he was last in Edinburgh, and he poured over these whenever he had a spare half hour. He was fascinated by what he was learning, and eager to put it to use.

*There are still those who'd think you're casting evil spells here,* he thought, *with your vials and your burners and the wood oven always fragrant with new and strange smells.* "Let them think it!" he challenged the smoke-stained walls. "They'll be glad in the end when I rid them of their pain or their illness or infection." But would they? he wondered. The churches did not approve of such experiments. It seemed to him Anglicans in 1820 were looking forward in a tried-and-true way, and the Presbyterians forward, while the Catholics clung to their Latin and their ancient Church. The people were letting go of their belief in the ancient Celtic gods, and the spells of the fey and the kelpies. They were letting go, too, of their history, a little at a time.

Magnus wasn't certain whether or not that was a good thing. *Ye think too much*, he told himself silently. "Better that than thinking too little," he said out loud.

# Chapter 5

*Several days later Esmé dreamed about a doe that radiated gentleness, a sense of healing warmth, and a connection to the verdant, fecund forest full of life. Even the rustle of water on stones had a voice and a breathing energy. On tiptoe, the girl followed the doe through copse and vale, over moor and brae and stream, up mountains and down fields alive with wild flowers. Esmé paused there and spun among the cotton grass and bluebells and twinflowers and creeping ladies tresses.* Spring will come again, *she thought,* and the winter disappear. *Somewhere inside, she sensed the dream foretold a new beginning, a rebirth, which filled her with euphoria and hope.*

*The dream was the vivid life and beauty and caress upon her skin. She felt she was not alone, though she could see no one about. She felt a strength protecting her—a hidden presence she knew in her body and her heart was male, full of yearning and dreams of his own. She was not safe, for the sense of his existence raced across her skin, awakening a need and a desire she had never felt before. And yet, somehow, she was not afraid. Instead she was starving for his touch, for the brush of his finger across her open lips.* Not now, *her heart whispered,* but soon. He will be there for you—waiting.

*For the longest time there was only stillness. And then The Voice began to whisper in her ear: to whisper of the Highlands many, many years in the past, to speak of the animals and how precious they were to the Gods, to speak of the Ancients and the Old Ways and the magic, of the power and the indescribable beauty—of the mist and gloaming and dawn and the strength of the changing sun. Of the time before when the Ancients had held sway.*

*And, caught up in the sweetness and the sovereignty of The Voice, Esmé listened, deep within a world beyond and before her own. A world where the dulcet tones of The Voice wove a pattern in the light, an invitation on the wall, a drawing in the tinted mist.* Come, *it said melodiously.* Find me. You will find what you seek only with me. *The words and the meaning were harmonious, in the soft resilience of The Voice, which reached for her, called for her, sang for her, the song that held her fast, clasped her close, released a million kisses upon her, and a deep yearning inside her, and it burst upon her skin like the music she could not hear, and upon her ears like a touch she could not feel. But she sorrowed for the voice of many colors and songs and strokes, and secrets she wanted to know that were deeply hidden. Forgotten as the world moved on.* The Voice has questions. It has a heart. It is missing; it misses, you. *She half-awoke in the darkness, yearning for something she'd once known but long forgotten: that rush of excitement in her blood, the desire for adventure, a touch upon her skin so light it was barely there, but so intense it made her burn—inside and out. Someone was there; his shadow fell across her as he reached out to offer his hand. Even before he touched her, her body was alive with desire, with heat, with longing. She tried to speak, but no sound came. She tried to move but felt she had been turned to stone.*

Esmé awoke standing outside the Hill in her night rail, barefoot and shivering. Every muscle in her body stiffened. "How…" she stuttered. "Why?"

*I told ye I would show ye the way*, The Voice whispered. *This is the first step.*

The girl stood unmoving, terrified, until her grandfather saw her through a window, rushed outside and whisked her up into his arms.

~ * ~

No one spoke of her inexplicable foray into the snow wearing her night rail. Everyone in the family knew it must have been a nightmare—the only thing strong enough to wrench Esmé from the safety of her bed into the treachery of the midnight snow. So her family waited to see if she mentioned what had happened. When she did not, they kept their questions to themselves.

"There's to be a small party tonight at the Hill," Breda informed her sister breathlessly. "And you're not to sit in the corner or be otherwise occupied."

Brow furrowed, Esmé replied, "I take pleasure in other people, Breda. Tis just the outdoors I'm no' very fond of. I always enjoy Grandmother and Grandfather's parties." She finished the last stitch in the hem of her pale lilac muslin gown. She had trimmed Breda's pale yellow one yesterday with some dainty gold lace. It lay across the bed in her sister's room, ready, Esmé suspected, for the party.

With an intensity Esmé had never seen in her sister before, Breda blurted out, "Ye must take a beau this very night. Ye simply must!" Breda was much the prettiest of the two sisters; at 16-years old, her strawberry blonde hair was thick and lustrous, and her sparkling golden eyes most striking. But just then, they were wide with determination, her rosy skin pale, and her grip on her sister's wrist tight.

Esmé was shocked by her apparent desperation. "Why must I?"

Breda rolled her eyes. "Because I can no' be betrothed until ye are married, and it'll take ye forever even once ye have a beau. I know ye, Esmé Rose Fraser." Breda pointed at her in accusation.

Putting her sewing scissors away in her basket, Esmé collected the snipped threads from her skirt and placed them in the small dish on her bedside table. She removed a piece of embroidery work she was doing as a gift for her grandmother and began to form the tiny colorful patterns of stitches. At last she sank into her four-poster bed and stared up at the pale green canopy while she worked. "Ye know I'm no' interested in looking for a man just now." She sighed, deeply immersed, for an instant, in the dream she *did* seek. The mysterious—something—she could neither name nor visualize, but which made her body quiver with sparks of anticipation.

"Exactly!" Breda stretched out beside her on the green duvet.

"Besides, you're too young to marry."

"You're not paying attention. It will take ye years to marry, even when ye do take a beau. You'd have to leave the house, for one thing," her younger sister pointed out practically, "and go live at his."

Esmé went pale and a tiny gasp escaped her. She felt her sister had struck her in the stomach. All at once she understood Breda's concern. She had not realized until that moment how much her fear of leaving the house affected the rest of the family. She had thought them all safe because she was taking no risks. But there was a different kind of risk in choosing security. She was hurt by her sister's matter-of-fact assumptions about how Esmé would hurt Breda's chances, and yet she wanted to apologize.

She wondered who else she had hurt by her hermit's ways, and how much they resented her for it. More than anything, she wanted, right then, to be back in the middle of the dream that seemed to cherish her. But that would be running away from the truth, and frightened as she was by the world beyond her door, that was one thing Esmé never did. She clasped the medallion in her hand and a faint, lingering warmth reassured her.

~ * ~

Perched on a stool in her grandmother's rooms on the top floor while Caelia sketched, Esmé breathed more easily. The girl had found comfort there, as she always did. The ceilings were sharply slanted with heavy carved beams to hold them up. The plaster walls were painted cream, but most of the space was taken up by the many-layered green ferns, starflowers, purple foxglove and rocks covered in lichen that Caelia had painted on the walls. A quite realistic image of a stream flowed over clear round stones, disappearing when it met the floor. Caelia had also added a small green pool, reflecting blue sky and clouds above the bed. She had done all that when she was only a girl. Esmé was also fascinated by the paintings and sketches and books piled on floor and tabletop. Somehow in this room, Esmé felt protected by her grandmother's 'gift'. The studio was across the hall, but the girl liked it here better. She even slept here sometimes when she was particularly restless.

"Whatever are ye thinking of, lassie?" Caelia asked after too much silence.

Despite her reluctance, Esmé glanced up. "Tis nothing. Just something Breda said."

Holding a black pastel in midair, her grandmother. "What could your sister possibly say to make ye look so baffled—and sad as well?"

Raising her chin as she gathered her courage, Esmé let out her breath on a long sigh. "If I ask ye a question, do ye promise to tell me the truth? Tis important." She looked down and toyed with the end of her braid.

"I've never yet lied to ye. Esmé, look at me. Why would I start now?"

Reluctantly, the girl met her grandmother's eyes. "Because, Grandmam, the truth might hurt me."

When she offered no further explanation, Caelia turned her sketchbook away. Esmé caught a glimpse of the sketch. The rounded face of a familiar woman with no detail, blowing question marks like bubbles. "Ye weren't really sketching; ye were waiting, were ye no'?"

Caelia nodded, her extraordinary golden brown eyes fixed on the girl. "I was. Waiting for ye to tell me what was on your mind. Come, join me. Ask me whatever ye like. If ye can't count on me to tell ye the truth, then you're lost indeed." She sat down on the bed, feet curled under her peach gown.

When Esmé had scrambled up beside her, nearly tearing her own white lawn gown with cap sleeves, she wasted no time. "Am I...is my behavior...the no' going out, is that hurting my family? Is it hurting ye?"

*Breda!* Caelia thought. *I'd like to shake the girl.* She took Esmé's hands and squeezed them.

Before her grandmother could answer, it all came tumbling out. "Don't be angry at Breda. She's just afraid it will be years and years before I marry, leaving her to become an old maid. Because I don't leave the house, ye see. She's afraid I'll never meet anyone, that I must choose a beau tonight. I mean, I've no care if she marries first, and I'm sure neither have ye, but she worries about Society. I can't imagine who she got that from. Anyway I realized I am hurting her as she sees things. I'd never thought of that, I am so blind. I thought by staying here I was keeping ye all safe. But I'm not, no' really, am I?"

Caelia was strangely quiet as she tried to absorb all this troubling information. "Esmé, *mo-cridhe*, I worry most that you're hurting yourself. I know you're not interested in any of the young men of our acquaintance, but mightn't ye learn to care for someone over time? Perhaps Peter or Angus? They're very serious young men, but they both know how to laugh."

Esmé was appalled that Caelia should make such a suggestion. The girl opened her mouth to respond and was shocked by what happened next. She shook her head vigorously, surprised by her own certainty.

Caelia was more than a little intrigued. "Why not?"

"Because there is someone for me already." The girl did not know where the words had come from, but somehow she knew they were true.

In her astonishment, Caelia gaped at her inelegantly for a moment. "How can you know that?" She was not incredulous, only curious—intensely so.

"I just do. From my dream." Esmé leaned back, looking about as if someone else had spoken.

Releasing her breath in a long "Ahhhh," Caelia settled back on the bed. This she could believe, just as she believed in the magic in the secret cave below the Hill of the Hounds, which many in Glen Affric had called Fairies' Haven for centuries. "Tell me about it."

"I don't know if I can. Tis no' something ye put in words, Grand. Tis just—" The girl closed her eyes, her face suffused with rapture. "I know he's out there somewhere. I wake up..." She licked her lips in discomfort and tried again, though she could not stop the color from rushing to her cheeks. "I wake up wanting him."

"Look at me, lassie."

Esmé shook her head.

"Don't fash yourself, Esmé, I've no wish to embarrass you. Look at me."

The girl raised her head, barely.

"You're a young woman now. Tis all right to want a man. But I'd no' be telling your grandfather or your father that I said so."

~ * ~

Breda flittered about among the guests in her yellow gown trimmed in delicate gold, her strawberry-blond hair half curled and braided on top of her head, half falling over her shoulder in long, loose coils. Every man there cast covetous glances her way.

Esmé watched, grinning to herself. She sat with the older and younger guests, as was her wont, entertaining the children while participating in the conversation with her elders.

"I haven't seen a winter this long ever," Grandda Rory

declared, his expression troubled. He kept his voice low so as not to disturb the young people enjoying themselves at the other end of the small ballroom, furnished more like a large, comfortable sitting room, with a fire roaring in the Great Hearth. "To be frank, I'm worried."

His son-in-law Connall nodded, and several others offered assent. Some remained silent, refusing to meet his eyes. "How are we going to raise enough barley and oats this year?"

"Aye, and the sheep and cattle have no grass to feed on."

*They're frightened*, Esmé thought. She could feel their dread as if it were her own.

"Tis a curse from a witch or The Darkness returning."

Esmé heard the whisper but could not tell where it had come from, though it echoed, spoken by more than one, and then fell silent. The girl believed there was something inherently wrong in the balance of Nature, but she kept that to herself. She also kept to herself her belief, hidden somewhere in her heart, that this winter would end and spring would come. Soon. She did not know how or why; she simply knew.

"If you're no' going to play games with us, will ye at least play music?" Geordie interrupted her thoughts. "Breda can dance and she'll stop scowling at us." The boy had learned the word 'scowling' just that morning when his older sister had accused her squirrel of scowling at her, and he was proud to use it in front of the adults. Before Esmé could respond, he pulled out his *cuiseach*—the hollow reed whistle she had made for him. "I can help," he said, his eyes full of hope.

"Of course ye can, Geordie." Esmé had left her flute behind the comfortable wingback chair for just such a moment. Her father took up the fiddle and her grandfather the Celtic drum. They began to play softly, building the music note upon note, until it swirled upon itself, filling the room with its cadence and melody. She was surprised to hear how well Geordie was keeping up; he must have been practicing.

"Well done, laddie of mine," Connall leaned down to whisper in his ear. "I believe ye share your sister's talent."

Geordie beamed and blew on his reed whistle all the harder.

At first the guests tapped their feet to the tune, then a few began to sway. Breda glowed when Angus MacKensie asked her to dance, and other couples took the floor.

The violin sang and prompted and demanded; the drum hummed, making skirts whirl and heels rise and fall; the flute danced hypnotically in harmony, wrapping Esmé just as tightly in its spell as it did the dancers. Angus swung Breda and she dipped and rose gracefully as naturally as if she had been doing this forever. Everyone watched the couple swaying over the wooden floor, spinning and bending like lovers who knew each other well.

Everyone had fallen silent, watching those two dance. Everything but Esmé's flute, weaving and interweaving notes into magic.

~ * ~

That evening Caelia painted in her studio while Rory watched in fascination. He never grew weary of seeing the images form and re-form under her colored pastels. He never knew where each painting was going to end, and neither did she.

"Tis Esmé," he murmured, afraid to break the spell she worked under. He squinted to try and puzzle out the vivid colors in swirls and arcs across the canvas. "But there's something different about her."

"Aye, *mo-charaid*," Caelia whispered, "she's growing beyond our ken, I think."

"Even yours?" Rory was incredulous. He regarded his wife in her deep blue dressing gown. Without ruffles or ribbons, it fell in simple elegant folds around her still slender body. She had let down her light brown hair, touched here and there with silver, and it fell down her back in a shining tumble. In the light of the oil lamp she looked young again, and wistful.

"Even mine," she said softly.

Hesitating because he did not wish to put his fear into words, Esmé's grandfather asked, "Will we lose her?"

For the first time, Caelia met her husband's eyes. "Ye want her to be happy, don't ye?"

"Of course I do. But will we lose her, beloved?"

Abandoning her painting, his wife sat on his lap, laying her head on his shoulder. "I don't know, Rory. We can only hope with all our hearts that she finds what she seeks without leaving us behind."

# Chapter 6

*Magnus dreamed, stumbling through the vivid green and gilded forest. The river flowed, glittering from flecks of gold on boulders piled one upon the other. The wind rushed through rowan, pine and birch, but water made no sound and the dancing leaves were silent. If anything, the beauty of moor and loch was more intense, more vibrant, but the music of the glen was gone. Instead he heard a new song— the rustle and murmur which at first he thought was water, and then realized was the faint shape of a woman moving through the trees, hands spread and drifting behind her as if to touch every leaf and pine needle and fern. No more than a shadow, she turned her head toward him, stopping beneath an oak that held her in its shade, caressed her as Magnus wished to caress her. He held his breath and reached for her—she with no real substance or features or beauty to seduce him. Nevertheless he found her alluring, enticing, irresistible. He was startled when she stretched her shadow arms toward him. He could feel her hunger in the vibration of her body; it echoed his across the veiled green stillness of the forest. His heart pounded in his ears and his lips tingled; he wanted to hold her, to kiss her gently so her shadow would not dissolve in his arms. He tried to move forward, smelling jasmine in the air and knowing she was the heart of that scent and his desire. He could barely breathe, he coveted her so much. The mist was falling, enveloping her in veils of white kisses, closing her away from him. Her head turned toward him once again; he saw her long shadow hair swing out behind her, and the mist whisked her away. Magnus leaned against a tree and tried to catch his breath.*

*And then a slow and quiet voice began to speak of*

*things beyond his ken. Things he felt he should have known but didn't. The Voice, so soft he could barely hear it, told him secrets of the Gods, of the Ancients and the Druids and before man's foot had touched the earth. It told him of the magic in the animals man used to worship, in rising and falling sun and moon—secrets of past and present, of future and of love. Of what mankind had lost as they gave up the old ways, of how magic had curled into itself and begun to disappear. Of the day that would come when he would be needed to help save what had been since time immemorial, and what would come to be.*

*He saw it all and understood, and was filled with hope and all the knowledge of the universe. And it was so immense that he could hardly take it in, though he had no doubt that all of this was true. He struggled to remember it, to lock it inside him so he would never forget again.*

*Because the dream was a promise and a threat, and the most amazingly beautiful thing he had ever experienced. So he clutched it close.*

And when the time came and he finally awoke, it was as if the dream had never been, and he remembered nothing.

Except that he was filled with longing. That he was empty and desired nothing more than to be filled. He finally thought long and hard about Julia, about how he'd loved her and the grief she'd left in her wake.

And then it came to him, like a whisper. *Will Julia fill the void inside ye, and answer your need? Or must ye seek your freedom and joy elsewhere—and far away?*

~ * ~

"The MacDonnells of Glengarry believe they're the kings of the earth because of their ancient name," Graeme pronounced, wide-eyed and full of energy at breakfast once again, and pontificating on his favorite topic of late.

Releasing a huge sigh of frustration, Magnus pretended

to concentrate on his cold meat and grilled bread.

"The name is *Domhnull*, ye might recall, if you've followed their history or ours." Diarmid directed this dour announcement at his oldest son. "It's the Gaelic and it means world ruler."

"I know very well what it means, Da," Magnus replied. "I've studied the Gaelic for years." He just managed to keep the sarcasm from his tone, but both brothers glared as if he'd poured it over their heads like hot oil. For the slightest moment he considered the possibility, biting his lip until it ached to disguise his grin. He had not yet made a decision about going to war over Julia MacDonnell's defection—or rather, his mind had been made up from the beginning, but he did not tell the three desperate men with whom he was sharing breakfast. They never let the subject drop when all four of them were together, which was why the laird—*at least for the moment*, he thought—tried to avoid that circumstance all together.

"The MacLeods of Lewis are supposed to be feuding furiously with MacDonnell of Glengarry," Hugh reminded his older brother in the tone of an irritated instructor who cannot make his student listen. "Have ye forgotten our great-grandmother was slaughtered and the family stash of gold stolen by a couple of MacDonnell scoundrels after the '45? I can still hear their war cry, 'The raven's rock!' echoing in my ears that day!"

"Aye, precisely so!" Graeme joined Hugh in his outrage.

Magnus forbore to mention that neither had been alive on that day, nor even close to it. His restraint made him choke on his beef.

"And what of the two boatloads of fish they made away with in my father's day?" Diarmid demanded, allowing his younger sons to refresh the rage he had allowed to wane over the past weeks.

"What of the cattle we took from them over these

many years?" Magnus asked calmly, though he was more than weary of the conversation. "Or the Jewel of Glengarry Grandfather robbed them of, though she was betrothed to another. Then he married her himself?"

"Tis a feud, mon. Tis what one does," Graeme answered, surprised that Magnus was so ignorant. "Besides, the MacLeods are the clan that's been insulted now. Tis our solemn duty to makes things right."

"They want to beggar us, that what tis," Diarmid added shrewdly. "Insult our honor, break a sacred oath, and steal that girl's dowry, beggaring us into the bargain with all the expenses we've put into the castle just to please the impatient lass."

Magnus jerked upright in his newly upholstered chair, which Hugh had demanded, along with all the other improvements in the dining room. Julia MacDonnell might not have been happy here, but she had never asked for better accommodations. However, it was true the cost of making the castle ruins livable was emptying their treasury far too quickly, and Julia's dowry would have helped the clan in an infinite number of ways.

"I'll tell ye what I'd do," Hugh whispered so loudly that the guard at the front gate could no doubt hear him.

"What's that?" Magnus inquired with little—if any—interest.

"I'd put every man I could on horseback, put a sword and dirk in his hand, and we'd thunder off to crush the MacDonnell of Glengarry in his keep."

"Aye!" Graeme was up in the middle of the room, sword in hand, swishing it viciously left and right. "Come, men! Don't ye want to root out these devils where they live? To catch them in their beds and slaughter them?"

Only a few servants lingered, waiting to see if the group needed more food or wine, but a gusty cheer went up as they grabbed their dirks and began to call for a raid. Even the women.

Magnus sighed again. He had expected as much. He knew all his brothers wanted to do was fight, and many a man would follow them, whether it had aught to do with the problem at hand or no'. It made them feel more masculine, he supposed, and braver and more useful. The problem was, it had nothing at all to do with repairing the breach between the MacLeods and the MacDonnells.

"In point of fact," he said in his quiet but firm voice, "I don't think the MacDonnell had anything to do with Julia running off. To crush him and his men would only excite more enmity and would in no way solve the trouble that faces us."

His father and brothers glowered at him resentfully. "How dare ye—" Diarmid began.

"Because tis the truth. Julia MacDonnell herself is the answer." *To our problems and to mine,* he added silently.

The room, though mostly empty of people was nearly full of war cries.

A small voice whispered in the laird's ear. "Will ye take me with ye when ye ride against the MacDonnells? Ye'll have wounds to sew up. Ye know ye will."

Magnus turned to glance at diminutive Sam, looking indistinguishable from a boy, with her hair pushed completely under her cap. He buried his head in his hands. Why had God blessed him with such morons for relatives? "I said we'll no' be going on a raid, Sam. We need to end the feud. The days of the great clan feuds are gone. We'd look like fools. Tis time for the clansmen to be taken care of, not hauled off to war at their laird's angry whim."

Sam frowned hugely. "I know, but tis nice to dream."

What kind of dreams did this young girl have, he wondered, and thought of his own, and shivered with unexpected pleasure. "Do ye even know the history of this feud?" he asked, more to distract himself than anything.

"Tis no' important. Tis just a fantasy."

For a moment, Magnus pictured Sam in the middle of a

melee. All a man had to do was to swing his shield wrong, and he could crush the girl's head. Yet she was excited and eager to go.

He'd had enough. He swigged down the rest of his wine, knocked the glass over when he set it down too hard, and went off to do some useful work.

No one paid him any mind.

# Chapter 7

*That night The Voice spoke in a whisper, cried in the fall of a crush of leaves, sang in an alluring song the reached out from the heart of her dream and bid Esmé come.* 'Come, I need ye. There is pain—great pain, and flames and the smell of burning flesh. I have no' the strength to fight all these things, and yet they are determined to fight me. Come'

*The vivid verdant greens and blues and yellows of the forest dimmed, then faded altogether, and the voice shouted—barely above a whisper—*'Come!' Ye are needed, little lost one. Come and help to bring the color back again, before it is burned to colorless ashes that have no color left to give. Come!'

*The protective shield was gone, and the veil, and the gauze; it was as if the deepest of Nature's secrets lay revealed to every eye and every foe.* 'Come! Help protect us from the unwise and the covetous, for we must keep our precious secrets and defend our solitary freedom. Come!'

*Esmé did not stir, she was listening so intently, feeling The Voice's pain, its fear, its vulnerability. She could not reject this plea, turn her back on this agony and turmoil. For this The Voice had chosen her; to this she must respond.*

'Come!' *The Voice sang in heartbreaking song,* 'for I will die without you. Come!'

*The Voice echoed in her soul so deeply that she rose as if following the notes, as if The Voice were her leash and her instincts the collar. She rose without hesitation, without thought, without fear and without question. The Voice needed her. She would go. She could make no other choice.*

*Yet she wondered, who spoke with such command, yet*

54

*softly, seductively? To whom did The Voice belong? The medallion glowed in her pocket, warmed her body, her legs, her shivering arms. She took it out and kissed it lightly, barely brushing it with her lips, and the glow from the circular piece lit her face.*

She awakened twisted in her night rail, her skin tingling, her breasts so sensitive that the fabric moving against them made her gasp. Her body ached and her need seemed as great as the need of The Voice, but she knew it was quite different.

She'd best be ready. In spite of all the arguments for staying safe in her familiar home, she would go. Not only for The Voice, which she had come to love, but because there was something else she was meant to find.

~ * ~

"By all that's holy, what is going on here?" demanded Rory MacGregor, when everyone came down for breakfast the next morning.

"I'm wondering the same," Connall Fraser, Esmé's father put in with rather less vigor.

Breda merely narrowed her eyes at her sister, while Grandmam Caelia sensed the tension in her eldest granddaughter and tried to unwind it.

Esmé had been up well before dawn, before even Cook awoke. She had brushed back her hair and braided it tightly, so it would not get in her way. She'd dug out her thickest pair of trews and warmest shirt, and a cap with which she could cover her hair, so she wouldn't look so obviously like a woman traveling alone. In addition, she had neatly folded her plaid, packed some of her herbs, some meat and dried berries. She had all this laid out on the work table.

"It looks as though you're taking a trip," Caelia observed blandly.

"Aye."

"She can't do that!" Breda turned to their father. "She's never even been outside! She's too frightened!"

Connall met Breda's gaze squarely until she sputtered and backed down.

"Well, at least, not in a while. And besides—"

"Esmé, lass," Caelia intervened, "where are ye going?"

Crossing her arms over her chest, Breda sulked.

Esmé opened her mouth, but realized she had no answer. "North?"

Her grandfather Rory decided he had waited long enough. "Are ye asking us, lass? If so, I might suggest ye do a wee bit more planning before ye worry about packing up yer things."

"But I have to go now, Grandda," Esmé insisted. "Tis urgent."

"At least tell us who you're going to see," Connall suggested.

Shaking her head as she flushed deeply, Esmé reached for a reasonable answer. But she was very bad at lying. Finally she shrugged. "I'm no' exactly certain. I just know they need me!" Her voice rose on the last few words.

Between bites of porridge, Breda stared at her sister in shock. "So ye haven't left the house since ye were nine, but you're going on a journey alone to see 'you don't know who' at 'you don't know where'. Is that about it?"

Esmé really did not enjoy being the center of attention. "I…well…

"Breda, lass, you seem to have finished your porridge. Why don't ye go get started with the horses?"

"But I want to hear—"

"I'm perfectly well aware of that. Nevertheless, off ye go.

Breda went off in a noisy huff.

"Esmé," her grandmother said, "do ye think ye could explain this more easily to me in private?"

The girl heaved a huge sigh. "Aye, Grandmam. Thank

ye."

"We'll take our tea into the sitting room then."

Before she knew what was what, Grandmother Caelia had whisked her away, closing the sitting room door behind them.

"Now come sit beside me and tell me everything."

Esmé hesitated, not because of Caelia, whom she loved dearly and trusted completely, but because the dreams were so much a part of her midnight private encounters that she felt she might be betraying a secret. She did not mind sharing the magic, because of her grandmother's odd version of the Sight. She was well aware she couldn't just speak with anyone about such delicate matters. *But Grandmam will understand, or at least try to. She will believe me.* So Esmé told her all about the dreams and The Voice and the call for help. She even took out the medallion and showed her how it glowed.

They sat on the settee together, letting their strong tea get cold. Caelia held her granddaughter's hands when she had finished. "Are ye sure tis a voice for good, and no' for evil?"

Esmé replied without hesitation. "Tis all that is good. There is no evil in it." She did not mention, however, what happened to her body, to her soul with each dream. She was naïve, but not a fool.

"Well then, I think ye must go. But I think we should send your father to protect ye."

Esmé took Caelia's hands and looked at her with great pity. "I will already be protected by the magic of the dream." She whispered the last word; it was not wise to speak it out loud when anyone might overhear.

"And how will ye find your way?"

"I will be shown." She held tight to the worn, ancient medallion, which had a strength all its own.

Caelia drew her granddaughter close in a tight hug. "Are ye sure you're ready for this?"

"Ye don't think I'm strong enough?" Esmé was stunned that her grandmother did not believe in her.

"Of course I believe in you. Of course ye are strong. Strong in spirit," Caelia murmured. "Strong in intention and in talent. But I wonder if you're no' afraid to use those things. Afraid of whom ye could be or where ye might end up?"

As always, Caelia saw too much. Frowning, Esmé pondered the question. "Just because I fear my future does no' mean I can abandon this quest. I have to go, Grandmam, others are counting on me. If tis difficult for me, then I must simply try harder. But I believe I have been preparing for this all my life. I just didn't know it. I was chosen for a reason." She straightened her chin. "The one thing I do know is that I'm ready now."

Caelia Rose had painted Esmé again and again and loved her like a daughter. Her own daughter, Sorcha, was much like Lila, Caelia's own mother. Sorcha could never stay still for long. She had come home to have her children, stayed for a bit, then left. So now that Esmé wanted to go, it broke Caelia's heart. She had thought the girl would always be there, was more like Caelia than Sorcha. "Are ye going for good?" Caelia could barely speak, she felt so bereft.

Her granddaughter seemed to understand all the thoughts that were running through the older woman's head. "I am Esmé, no' my mother. Only that. And I promise I will come home to you." She didn't know how she was so certain of this, but she was. She squeezed her grandmother's hands. "I promise."

Their eyes met, Esmé's shining with tears and an honesty Caelia could not doubt. "I know my mother promised, but I am not her. As I said before, I am Esmé. Please trust me."

With difficulty, Caelia kept the tears from her eyes. "I do, *mo-run*. I'm trying."

Smiling that secret smile of hers, the girl put her hand

on her grandmother's cheek, and her palm seemed to draw all the flushed pink into itself, while her fingers cooled and soothed.

Tears shimmered in Caelia's golden-brown eyes. She had never seen her granddaughter look so confident or determined. And yet she was so slight, fragile. Caelia's heart constricted in her chest. *Esmé is not ready*, it cried. *You must stop her from this madness.* But she knew she could not; somehow this time had come upon her and she was needed. Esmé had been chosen.

Her grandmother was both proud and petrified, but she was also determined not to make the young girl doubt herself. Doubt could destroy any good she might do. More than anything, Esmé must believe with all her heart and soul.

# Chapter 8

It was the oddest thing. The more Magnus dreamed, the less concerned he became with the factions within his clan. He could see quite clearly they were bored, and he put as many as he could to work shoring up the castle walls, building new ones, bringing in stones for the wall around the moat, and making the intact chambers more livable. It was a wise decision, though he was well aware no one would ever call him Magnus the Astute. Still, he was determined they would not call him Magnus the Foolish.

He continued his healing duties while overseeing the plans for re-making the castle, but he was restless, impatient, as though he were waiting for something he knew nothing about.

"Are ye goin' to be growlin' at me today again?" Sam asked flippantly. "Because if ye are, I might as well go home and let my father do it."

Magnus looked up in surprise. "Growl at ye? Why on earth would I do that, lass?"

Her eyes widened. "Because tis the only way ye talk to me lately. I'd begun to think ye'd forgotten your words."

"Don't be ridiculous! You're exaggerating, just like ye always do!" he said with a wee bit more force than he intended.

Hands on hips, she faced him squarely. "Is that so?" Sam was angry herself now, tired of explaining away all his little slights and rudenesses. "Well, then, I'll take myself from your hearin', since my voice is so calamitous." Just like that, she disappeared.

Staring at the place where she had been a moment past, Magnus realized he was frowning fiercely. Sam was right; he was behaving like an ogre, or a MacDonnell, as Hugh would have said. Something was weighing heavily on his mind, and he did not want to admit it might have anything to do with the promise of the dream, which was given again and again, only to be taken away as often. He ached with that lost promise, and that was something he would not confess to anyone.

~ * ~

*That night the dream swallowed him whole. Magnus fought it at first, but the pull was too strong. It attacked his body, from the top of his head to the soles of his feet, with music that pulsed through his heart and his veins, so he throbbed with each note and rose, full of sensation, with each crescendo. The reed whistle danced along his skin like an invisible caress, while the strings of the hand harp followed, plucking, sliding, skimming along his torso with the skill and the rapture of angels.*

*When his body sang out for release, the music subsided, and he heard The Voice—strong but imperative. It called to him as a siren would, like the beauties who crooned the great warships of old onto the rocky shores, where they were wrecked and all their treasures and their manhood taken.*

*It urged him in the tone of a warrior, ready for battle, ready for blood, ready for victory at any cost.*

*It prevailed on him as warriors prevailed on their destriers to carry them, and their armor to safeguard them.*

*It begged him as a younger brother begs his older laird for just one night of battle.*

*It called to him in a manner he understood, and he knew that he must follow.*

*Though when he woke, he ached and felt hollow and alone. Except that this time, he felt hope in a flame beneath his skin that burned with wanting and need, and the knowledge that someday soon the wanting and need would be over.*

~ * ~

In the morning, Magnus appeared at breakfast, freshly shaved, face and hands washed and wearing a clean shirt, waistcoat and breeches. He smiled, first at Diarmid, then Graeme and then Hugh.

"I'm glad you're all here," he told them with warmth and suppressed excitement. "I've decided what I'm going to do about the crafty MacDonnells of Glengarry.

All three stared at him expectantly.

"I shall take it upon myself, as Laird and ruler of the MacLeods, to go in search of Julia, my betrothed, and I swear I'll no' return here until she is by my side."

They shouted; they ranted; they complained and made speeches. But in the end there was nothing they could do. They had demanded he solve the problem and he was going to do so. They could groan because it wasn't what they wanted, but they certainly could not stop him.

As he left the dining room, Magnus smiled to himself. He had made them believe it. He almost believed it himself.

# Chapter 9

She had said she was ready, had even believed it. The traveling pack hung off one arm and down her back, full to bursting, and she had hugged and kissed even her pouting and disbelieving sister. Then Grandfather Rory opened the front door, and Esmé stood paralyzed. She had not looked out and down at the snow-covered ashes, rowans, pines and beeches, the ferns in winter sleep along the loch, the cotton grass, crushed and dead beneath snow and horse hooves and wagons and plows. She had not touched the door handle or leaned against the heavy mahogany for nine years, and she most assuredly had never stepped outside.

Her throat began to close and her heart to race. She pressed her hands to her chest because she could not breathe. Her face turned red and she grasped her chest with both hands.

"Someone close the cursed door." It was Breda who shouted, who slammed the door shut, who hurried Esmé to a chair and offered her hot tea and sugar. "Just breathe, Es. Just remember to breathe."

Esmé nodded mutely, surprised she could accomplish that much. She was grateful beyond tears for her sister in that moment. Esmé herself had not known what to do.

Gradually her pulse slowed, though not to its normal rate, the room steadied and the swelling in her throat went down, leaving her quite nearly normal. Clinging desperately to her medallion, she remained silent for a long time.

Her family gathered around the table in silence, waiting for her to speak first, not wanting to shatter her fragile protective shell. But they did not understand Esmé. No one did, except for Breda.

"I'm all right now. Mostly," she announced at length. "I'll try it again in a little while, but ye needn't wait here for me."

"But Esmé—"

"Are ye sure that's wise—"

"Perhaps ye should postpone your trip—"

She tilted her head to get a better view of their concerned faces. "Ye weren't listening before. I have to go, and I have to go soon—now. So I will conquer this fear, because I have to. Now, today."

Her expression was not angry or irritated, but rather the look of a girl who simply wants to be understood.

Everyone wanted to say more—except for Breda—but everyone refrained. They went off to follow their own pursuits. Except for Breda.

"Thank you," Esmé said. She was bundled up in a warm flannel shirt and trews, her plaid, a woolen sweater and a heavy greatcoat. She was getting overwarm but was still too shaken to think straight.

"Here," Breda told her, "let me takes those things. No point in getting over heated too."

For some reason, Esmé found that inordinately funny. Both girls laughed a bit too much in relief and at the thought of repeating the effort.

Once they were alone, Breda looked thoughtful. That was unusual enough for Esmé to ask, "What?"

"Do ye ever miss mam? Tis just, when I saw ye out there, I had a thought about her always going away."

Esmé took her sister's hand. "*Ye* miss her, don't ye? Sometimes I do, sometimes I'm just curious and sometimes—"

"I hate her!" Breda interrupted.

Esmé shook her head sadly. "I always think one shouldn't do that. Tis hurtful for ye as well as her. But yes, sometimes I wonder if we would be less confused if we knew her better?"

"Confused about what, Es? I'm no' confused. I'm just angry. Ye should be too." Breda's cheeks were flushed, then pale, then flushed.

Esmé wanted to comfort her, but had no idea how. "I can no' let myself be angry. If I did I'd be angry all the time."

Leaning in close, her sister whispered, "Perhaps ye are and ye just don't know it."

Brushing the thought away like a persistent insect, Esmé refused to think about it. "I think she's sad."

"But she doesn't care, Es. Ye know she doesn't. Yet you're not afraid of that are ye? Is there nothing you're no' afraid of?"

Esmé bowed her head in shame. She was trying to be brave that day, but she was terrified. Perhaps, after all, she did hate Sorcha Fraser. She couldn't help it. Here she was, burdened by guilt from things that had happened long ago, and her mother never felt guilty at all. Not one little bit. She just left them behind without a glance, without a last minute kiss, without anything to show them she loved her children. Because she didn't. Esmé was certain of it. But she did not tell Breda that.

~ * ~

After four tries, Esmé finally inched her way outside the Hill of the Hounds. With her sister close beside her, holding Breda's hand and shivering all the while, she paused. *Don't think,* The Voice reminded her. *Only feel the things your heart tells you—and your soul, for they are pure.*

She felt it first in the pit of her stomach, so she summoned up The Voice and the music from her dreams, and with them came the courage she needed to take more steps away from the house, one by one, until, after what seemed like hours, she could no longer see the house, or her sister waving solemnly.

Esmé still felt sick, but it occurred to her for the first time that she had not really believed she could do this, but maybe she could after all. Maybe.

~ * ~

Later, after she had walked all day among the piles of snow and the grass and flowers trying to break free of winter's grasp, while carrying on a nonstop conversation with the woodland animals and The Voice to keep herself amused—and to inform whoever might be interested why she was there. She realized she'd begun to ache all over, and it was time to start looking for a place to stop for the night.

She had already run across several men on various errands in the forest, and she was glad to be dressed as a boy, which kept her out of certain kinds of danger. She passed a rickety Inn that and decided against it as soon as she poked her head in and took a whiff. It smelled of urine and unwashed bodies and smoke and ale. Not her favorite fragrances.

She decided to keep looking. Taking out the medallion, she saw it was glowing; she followed that glow to a clean little croft where the dwellers were willing to let a traveler stay. She wanted to save by eating her own food, but the woman had burned her hand while cooking a thick brose on the fire in the middle of the room. Esmé offered to help.

She gave the woman some chamomile tea to calm her, then gently applied garlic balm on the burn itself to both soothe the pain and keep it from becoming infected.

Amazed by the results, the old man and his son and especially the woman, asked her to share their meal. She could not refuse without being rude, and besides, she was starving. So they all sat down to beef brose and flat bread. Watching the firelight dance across the three faces of the strangers, Esmé felt as if she knew them somehow.

She slept dreamlessly on a plain straw pallet and arose

feeling rested and revived. She changed the dressing on the woman's wrist, making sure she left behind some chamomile and garlic balm. In return, they gave her crowdie and fresh bannocks.

All three stood in the doorway watching her go, smiling, glad she had come. It was a strangely pleasant feeling. It made her feel stronger somehow—or was it only less afraid?

She had gone no more than half a mile when she realized she had no idea what direction she should take. She stopped still, confused, and the aches returned to her body. *Odd*, she said to herself, *I'd not even noticed they were gone. But what do I do now?* She spun in circles, desperation rising, hopelessly disorienting herself, until she was exhausted. *Listen to your instincts. Silence your thoughts.*

The words were so clear she was sure someone had spoken them out loud right beside her. She stopped, suspended in the suddenly falling mist, and touched the medallion. It glowed in only one direction. Concentrating on that area, where pine trees clustered at the edge of a forest, Esmé noticed an unusual thing—an old crone in a dark cloak, disappearing into the woods.

Without knowledge or intention, Esmé turned to follow her.

# Chapter 10

Magnus was grateful for the new morning; he liked the scent of the pine and spruce woods, and chopped wood for his fire with great satisfaction.

"Magnus, ye are very good at chopping wood," he said to himself. It was too quiet out here on the trail he was following by instinct. "No green pieces in here, they're all of a size, and will burn quite nicely. Well done, lad."

"Were ye talkin' to me, laddie?" an unfamiliar voice asked.

Magnus stepped back the slightest bit, startled by the sudden appearance of an old crone in a dark cloak. Her eyes sparkled with mischief. "Well, were ye?"

"Ahh...no, as it happens. Just trying to fill the silence."

The old woman tilted her head, considering. "But isn't that why a body comes to a place like this? To enjoy the silence?"

She was grinning at him and he could not understand why. "I suppose tis pleasant—"

"Or are ye waitin' for someone?" She cackled and he took offence.

"Well, I'm right, am I no'? No point in gettin' snippy about it." She began to shuffle through the enormous pockets in her cape. "I had a message for ye, but what was it? The broken crown? No. The secret pact? No, that was the couple in the Hebrides. Och! I remember now. I'm to remind ye that when ye meet her, she's so strong ye'll think she's invincible. But she's fragile too. Look with different eyes, me lad. Different eyes will do it."

With a flap of her cape, she disappeared.

Magnus was left completely bewildered. "But who—? What—?"

He stood with his mouth hanging open, looking very much like a large, confused fish.

~ * ~

By the time she found a place to stop and camp for the night, Esmé was exhausted. The oak, near enough a stream that she could get to water, was wide and tall, its branches spread in a leafless canopy over the peat and the red mud by the burn. Esmé dropped her bag, carefully removing her tight-wrapped package of bannocks and sweet rolls and fistfuls of dried meat.

She observed the tree closely and finally found a knot she was sure she could use to climb up to the seat of the branches, where she could leave the food for the night—out of the reach of animals. She boosted herself up, clinging to the trunk, when she heard a growl behind her.

Freezing as she had done once before in her life, she heard the growl grow closer and ever closer. She was too terrified to face the beast, for she feared she knew what it was, but even in that deadly moment her curiosity was uncontrollable. Esmé turned her head the tiniest bit and found herself face to face with a huge old bear. Reaching out for her packet of food, it stood so close she could feel its breath on her face. Time seemed to stand still as she glanced down and saw an old wound track along its hip and leg. Her heart, which had stopped beating, began to pound again.

For a reason she could not understand, she stared into the great bear's face, directly into its eyes. Her gaze seemed to hypnotize it, but only briefly; the bear roared its most fearsome snarl.

Esmé did not look away. She simply stared, her silver-grey eyes steady.

Strangely, the bear did the same.

Finally breaking out of her trance, the girl threw the food as far as she could. When the bear followed the food, she slid down the tree and took shelter in a hollowed out space on the far side. But the bear did not return. It had what it wanted.

Esmé sat in the hollow for hours, knees pulled tightly to her chest, shivering, but not from the cold. She did not think she would ever breathe normally again. When the moon had set behind the trees, she crawled inch-by-inch to the burn and washed her body and her hair, both of which smelled like bear to her. *The* bear. She knew without a flicker of a doubt the beast had been the one that attacked her father. The one that had tried to make her choose. It could have killed her this time. But it had not even tried. The question that rang in her head like an ever-ringing church bell was *why*? *Why* had it let her live? She simply could not understand.

~ * ~

That night she did not fall asleep until quite late. For hours she grasped the tree in stiff fingers, afraid to let it go. *But when the dream floated across her eyes, she felt tranquil and satisfied and hungry for something—or someone—she did not know. She was in a pool surrounded by tilted boulders and warm flat rocks of gold and green and shades of rust. Above, a glittering waterfall tumbled over a steep drop in the river.*

*Sliding her feet over the smooth stones beneath the golden water, she released her hair from its braid and leaned back so it fell into the cool, refreshing water. Above, the trees made a canopy of light and shadow, light green, mid-green, forest green, always moving, always changing with the dappled yellow sunlight. She closed her eyes and conjured music as easily as she conjured magic in the flowing, tinted air.*

*All at once, she knew she was not alone. She turned with the river water rippling around her, stroking her naked skin. Shivering with delight, she saw a tall man made of vines intertwined with narrow branches and rolled green ferns. She could not mistake the shape or the intention of this man. He was moving toward her slowly with his face made of fern tips; she thought fleetingly that she ought to be frightened, but she knew there was no danger here.*

*At least no ordinary danger.*

*Esmé swayed and the water spread around her in circles that finally reached the man and drew him ever nearer. He caught her motion and copied it, and soon the pond was broken with a hundred widening circles. She thought he smiled, though he had no real features so she could not tell.*

*Then came the moment when they stood waist deep across from one another. She wanted to reach out and touch him, but something physically held her back. She wanted to kiss him through the invisible barrier between them. Leaning forward, she pressed her lips to a misty veil, pretending it was his lips. And when their mouths met, it was oh, so sweet, so tender, such a promise and a revelation. They stood together but apart, enwrapped by the water, not touching, sometimes not seeing one another through the mist. The sensations that rolled over and through them were electric, melting, and enchanted.*

# Chapter 11

Magnus went hunting the next day. He walked and crouched and listened and sniffed but had no luck, until a strange wind flapped by, dislodging some rocks and revealing some wild sheep high up on a hillside, sheltering under a huge flat rock. He could see they were not doing well, so he gave them some grain he had brought along and dragged some water near. One however, had split its back hoof, probably on a sharp rock, and deep infection was already setting in. It would die soon and in great pain.

He saved it from that, and himself from hunger. He sat for a long time beside the fire, considering how lucky he had been in general his whole life, brothers and Julia notwithstanding. For the first time he admitted to himself that he had not come in search of the wandering MacDonnell woman. He had come at the behest of The voice.

He slept unaccountably well that night, and in the morning ate well again. He was about to discard the remnants, which were plentiful, when a high-pitched voice stopped him.

"Just what do ye think you're doin', lad?"

Magnus knew without looking that the old crone was back. "Cleaning up after myself," he said, incensed by her accusing tone.

"Wasting perfectly good meat, it seems to me." She regarded him disapprovingly, her eyes narrowed to slits. "Healers should know better," she intoned.

"What am I to do with it, then? I'm certain you have a suggestion."

The crone shivered. "Tis cold out the day, and the river's even more frigid, I'll be bound. Ye could leave it underwater to preserve it, in case another traveler comes along."

"Another traveler?" He pointed all around at the silent, winter bound landscape with only patches of grass and mud and wildflowers here and there. "Who would be daft enough to travel to a place like this?"

The woman tilted her head in reply, tilting her forehead at him.

Magnus threw his hands up in despair. "Aye, weel, you're right about that." *Why are ye talking to her anyway? She just a figment of your imagination?* Yet he still felt guilty.

"Look here," he demanded, "what is your name, in case I see ye again."

She rubbed her chin between two fingers, considering whether or not to answer. "Gertrude." She stood with arm crossed as if waiting for him to bow as if she were royalty.

"Och, no! Tis ye who should bow to me," he growled.

"Then tell me this—if I abandoned ye out of spite, how, exactly would ye find yer way?"

Magnus chose the wise path and did not answer. Instead he dragged the meat to icy river, tying it to a rock and muttering all the way. "Waste of time. Complete waste of time. Another traveler. Bollocks."

~ * ~

Esmé was starving when she reached a good camping place two days later. She was too proud and too ashamed to ask for food at the cottages she passed, and there had been none for a long time now. Besides, the medallion had not told her to stop. Until now. "I wish I'd overcome my pride and asked," she said out loud. That's what Grandmam would have done." She alternated talking and playing her flute to keep herself company. She had never been so lonely in her life, except, of course, in her dreams, when she was never alone.

She dropped her bag among the long twisted roots of the tree and went to examine the fire. The stones and the ashes were cold; the fire had gone out long ago. Esmé was disappointed and her belly growled, especially when she stirred the ashes and raised the smell of meat. But there was really nothing left; the juices must have dripped into the fire. Standing, she rubbed her temples where her head ached terribly. "I never get headaches," she said. "It's the hunger and weariness and the aching." She was trying not to complain, but she thought it must be all right if no one was around to hear her.

Just then she noticed a thin trail of blood leading to the river. "Probably just the offal," she told herself so she wouldn't be disappointed. Kneeling on the bank, she leaned forward and was overjoyed to find the meat of a lamb tucked under peat and rushes. Weak with relief, she lifted it out and began, unaccountably, to cry.

Esmé had sounded brave when she explained this to her grandmother, but the truth was, she did not quite believe she would be guided to her mysterious location, that she would be protected, that it was urgent she do as The Voice asked. She'd believed, momentarily, that the bear might kill her, that she'd not find her way, that she had no strength to go on such a journey. She had even believed she would starve.

She was astonished to realize that somehow she had survived it all, alone, frightened and inexperienced. She could not help but smile at whoever had left this meat for the next traveler to come along. Because she knew full well that without it, this would have been the end of her journey.

She did not wonder about The Voice and what it needed from her, because she knew she could never guess. That one mystery she would have to leave in other hearts and others souls until the time was right. As she ate, her excitement rose again. She hoped she could do whatever it was. She did not assume she could; she had failed too many times for that. But maybe, just perhaps, this time she would succeed.

~ * ~

*In Magnus's dream, he was following a hind, his bow ready, arrow within reach. The deer led him deeper and deeper into the forest, until it became a rough wilderness where the ferns grew as tall as his shoulders and the moss climbed the craggy boulders beside the passionate rush of the river. He felt he knew this place, though he was certain he had never been there previously. The shapely trees breathed in, and on their outward breath came a call to his heart, which before had been shielded. He sighed in both pleasure and sorrow as the ferns brushed over his arms and legs, clinging only slightly, drawing out the soft, giving side he never showed. All around the living things took on the feel and scent and fire of women. He glanced up and the clouds formed vessels, and everywhere he looked there was seduction and desire.*

*Magnus thought of the shadow woman and suddenly she was near but just beyond his reach. In the instant he saw her, his bow disappeared, and the arrows hanging from his back. He was defenseless against her slender, ethereal form, but she moved gently, and he could not resist. He held out his arms with a silent cry, and The Voice cried out too, calling and calling.*

*The shadow woman stood a breath away from him: hip to hip, toe to toe, arms to arms and lips to lips. So very, very close, but so, so far away. He could not cross that tiny space between them, nor could she. Still he felt he was touching her, kissing her, her lips parting under his, shaking him so deeply that he almost lost his balance.*

Come to me, Magnus! Only you can help me. You are chosen. You and the other. Come! *For an instant more he lingered, then turned away from the promise and his craving and her undefined beauty.* He awoke with tears on his cheeks. He could feel her hair around his face and shoulders; he was aroused, hungry, had been too long without a woman. "This woman is different," he said, as if to make it so. "More alluring by far because I can see into her dreams. I can kiss her in my dreams."

At last he woke up fully, lying deep in fresh snow. "Ridiculous!" he shouted, fighting back the images which had held him in thrall. And yet—and yet. He felt he knew this dream woman as he had never known Julia. He could not tell what she was thinking, which is why it was so easy for her to lie, and for him to believe. She did not fill him, or rid him of the ache and the darkness.

Of course it was not Julia calling him; she could never have touched him so deeply on the wound he neither admitted to having nor showed to others. Yet The Voice seemed to both rip the scab off that wound and promise healing—and something more. Far more.

He took out some strips of dried beef and gnawed on them as he packed up his pointed leather bag and continued on his way north.

# Chapter 12

Magnus woke abruptly, his heart pounding so hard he could not catch his breath. His dark hair covered his face and his eyes were closed, so he could not see—did not wish to see. He knew when he opened them it would be there: the challenge, the final effort on this lengthy, confusing journey.

He sat for a long, painful time, waiting for the thunder in his chest to cease, for his breath to come more easily, but nothing changed. Finally, in resignation, in anticipation, in fear that he would not be enough for what he had to face, he opened his eyes and swept his hair back.

A winter world, frozen from end to end, lay stretched before him: jagged mountain peaks and slick frozen lochs; white, glittering snow nearly covering the evergreens of spruce and cedar—the ends of the branches the only color in sight.

How had he gotten here? He did not remember climbing so high or hiking through ice and over slippery rock. Magnus glanced back to discover the same world of winter behind him: glass-topped mountains, frozen rivers stopped half rush, an infinite forest of evergreens. It was pristine, untouched, with no footprints or broken rocks to show his passing. "Because," he said out loud, "I did not come that way."

And yet, here he was. He held his hand above his eyes to block out the sun and peered across to the mountains that rose in the distance. He did not know how he was to get there, but he knew that was where he must be. He tried to stand, knowing he would fall—but he managed to stay upright. He was wearing the strangest looking things on the bottom of his boots. Inside a tautly curved and braided leather, someone had woven tight strings back and forth, under and over in a diamond pattern. The bizarre woven things were tied over top his boots.

Magnus grinned and took a step. He did not sink into the crystalline snow, but stayed steady on top. All this was impossible, but he did not have time to worry about it. *Hurry, hurry, hurry,* the weak voice urged him.

He grabbed his bag, tossed it over his shoulder and started off toward the twin ice mountains in the distance.

# Chapter 13

*Esmé was lost, drowning in the unkind waters of the loch. The pain radiated through her tiny body, wracking her bones. She tried to close her eyes against the flames leaping among the lochs near-frozen waves, but she could not escape. The heat grazed her delicate skin, marring it, puckering it with a throbbing that would not cease. All at once a jagged-edged stone was heading for her and she froze, unable to move, as it sliced her deep across the chest. Her blood flowed into the icy water, billowing into the choppy flames: weeping, stinging, singing out in anguish.* I am here! Help me! I need you!

~ * ~

Esmé woke up gasping in torment and grief. "Tis too late!" she cried to a motionless, emotionless world. "Again!" She stretched out on the snow, reaching for something or someone she believed she could never have. *Not too late*, the voice murmured. *Don't ye give up on me. Don't.*

Sitting up, Esmé felt the warning like a fist shoved into her stomach. "I don't give up. I'm strong. Grandmam Caelia said so. *Strong in spirit*, Caelia declared in her memory. *Strong in intention and in talent. But I wonder if you're no' afraid to use those things. Afraid of whom ye could be or where ye might end up?*

The girl squinted as though in pain. Why had she not heard and understood the first time? Her grandmother was right, as was The Voice.

She did give up. Always. That's why she had hidden away in the house for so long; why she had learned the healing arts, but never taken them out to help the people;

79

why she turned young men away without looking—they might challenge her heart, her protected soul, and leave her defenseless once more. Because she *had* given up. She was too afraid to risk losing one more thing.

The knowledge burst inside her, bright as the rising sun on the smooth white snow, trailing lilac, purple, pink clouds, and the color stained the pristine landscape for those few minutes, then was gone. But Esmé's burst of light would never go. It consumed her.

Yet she had no time to sit and wonder at the magic of the light. She had to go, to get to The Voice before it flickered out. Gathering her things, she rose, barely noticing the strange-shaped laced objects tied to her boots. She concentrated on the pain that drew her forward across the winter landscape—the beautifully frightening icescape so far from the home she loved.

And then she came up short against a solid wall of stone that rose straight up into the sky. To her left she saw one after another waterfall frozen solid in mid-current—not one drop of water fell from these ice behemoths, but they glittered and shimmered in the sun that did not warm.

Esmé forgot the impossible-to-climb stone wall. She forgot her fear of an everlasting winter. She was mesmerized by the beauty and unlikelihood of those waterfalls of ice, and the white silent world around them.

"Not yet," a voice above her interrupted. "Ye've work t'do, m'lassie."

Looking up, the girl saw the same old crone she'd glimpsed before, standing sideways on the rock wall, several feet above her head.

"Follow me," said the woman of few words.

Only then did Esmé notice that the wall was not a wall, but a natural stone incline. The lower part went back and up, so, determined to get to the top in time—

"Yes, tis to the top ye're going," the crone confirmed, making the girl more nervous, rather than comforting her.

Esmé doggedly climbed, often clinging to little more than a slight out-cropping of stone. She was sweating, and her breath kept catching in her throat; this was not what she was used to. Having spent so much of her life inside, she was not sure she was strong enough. Her body had let her down before.

"Tis yer soul that's strong, sweet lassie. Stronger than I've seen in a long, long time. Yer body will follow where yer soul leads. And yer soul knows where it's goin'."

The crone was no longer laughing. Esmé gave herself up to this new voice (praying to the Tuatha Dé Danann that it was not the voice that had called her here), and stopped thinking and wondering.

Slowly, painfully, inch by inch she climbed the wall, scraping her arms and legs, hitting the side of her head, but never once taking a step backwards or letting go. It took her many hours, and once, as she stared behind the waterfalls, she thought she saw a figure—a man—making the same climb, but she shook her head and when she looked again, he was gone. For reasons she could not explain to herself, she was inordinately disappointed.

But she did not have time to worry over it. Her sense of urgency was greater and greater, and she hurried faster, climbing over the top at last, but slipping back and cutting her leg on a sharp rock. "Bollocks!" She glanced around. Up here it was the same: perpetual winter, except for the trail of her blood in the snow.

# Chapter 14

Spitting and sputtering, Magnus climbed the last few impossible feet of the impossible rock face. His clothes were stained and torn, his boots battered as if he'd been wearing them for years. He checked the soles, where at least two holes were working their way through. "Bollocks!" he shouted to the cold in general and The Voice specifically. He thought he heard an echo down the way, but that could not be in this vast flat winter wasteland.

And then he saw two things. The woman and the flames.

Esmé caught sight of him, and in the next instant smelled fire. Her heart raced. This was it—the end of the long journey she had taken, the things she had learned, the possibilities. As if drawn by a magnet, she and the man began walking away from the rock face and toward each other—and the distant crackle and smell of fire.

When they reached each other, they stood staring, silent, stunned. Magnus was tall, and though not precisely handsome, his chiseled features were compelling. His shoulders were broad enough, but not too broad, and his body honed, though not like a soldier's. His hands were intriguing with their long fingers, and the expression on his face, though irritated, hid some other emotion entirely. Esmé's thoughts and feelings were jumbled: full of joy and expectation and recognition overtop her fear and pain and sense of dread.

"So, not Julia," he muttered, knowing only in that moment that he'd guessed it all along. Knowing also that he did not care. She was lovely, this girl-child, with her heart-shaped face and long blond hair. Her silver-grey eyes both reflected and obscured the winter landscape; they were full to the brim of wisdom and a kind of ache he had never seen before.

"Do I know ye?" she asked.

"I think no'. That is—mayhap."

She summoned all her courage and told him, "I'm Esmé. I was brought here by a dream."

"I too. By a dream. I am Magnus." *You're not mad, Magnus,* he rejoiced internally. *And the yearning—surely it's for her.* They could not be so cruel as to lure him here with the shape of her, the taste of her, the image of her just beyond his reach... *But you're getting ahead of yourself. Acting the fool again. You don't even know her.* But he felt, deep inside, that she was familiar in a way he had known no other.

She offered her hand and he took it, clasping it tight as flashes of emotions, intensity, tenacity went through their bodies.

Shivering from the aftermath, he said, "We have work to do."

"To the fire," she replied.

They began to run wordlessly over the soft silent snow that once again seemed to go on forever. Then, all at once, the fire came into view, and above it the image of the celestial white buck, shimmering palely, guiding the way. They paused for only an instant, dazed by its beauty, by its very existence, for both had heard stories of such a great being—white from head to toe, its antlers huge and glowing with heavenly light as it rose above the snow. A beacon of hope, of honor, of nobility, and protection. Beneath it, the fire had melted a ring of snow, obliterating the trees, singeing the grasses. And something lay in the center of that deadened ring.

Esmé's heartbeat and hurting were greater as she raced awkwardly through powder, then over ice where the flames had melted the snow and it had re-frozen, she slid at last into the barren circle, not warm and yet not chilly. She knelt beside the stricken animal. It was a white fawn—a tiny baby fawn—with burns on part of its side and back, and someone had cut it across. Beside it lay a sharp rock, on edge, coated with blood.

Esmé remembered her dream and shuddered. With great care, she lifted the fawn's head and rested it in her lap. *Ah,* The Voice said inside her. *At last you have come. I will rest now while you heal me.*

"But why me?" She glanced up at the man, at Magnus, whose presence confused and aroused her. "And why him?"

*You need not speak aloud. I can hear you. You two were chosen from the beginning, from my birth, because together, you can save me.* The voice was fading, and Esmé knew she must work fast. The fawn was frightened, its pulse racing, and its injuries were serious, so Esmé brought out an infusion of chamomile in one of the jars her grandmother had helped her prepare, which would calm it and help keep down the swelling. She had worked on small wounds, but none as severe as these. She knew if she gave way to her terror, the fawn would feel it too, so she took a bit of the infusion herself. Then she took out her recorder and began to play soft, soothing music that wrapped its tendrils—like the green tendrils of new growth at spring— around the fawn, and around her, and even Magnus, whose pulse slowed as he beat back the fire, stifling the flames with snow until gradually he separated them one by one and they sizzled out in the snow.

When Magnus knelt beside the fawn he was vastly discouraged. How could he help an animal so tiny and so helpless? So badly wounded?

*Think,* The Voice urged him. *You know what to do.* He glanced at Esmé and she smiled for the first time and nodded.

"I'm too big. I'm afraid I will injure it further."

"Here," Esmé whispered, "take my hand." She placed

her palm just above the fawn's open wound, and Magnus rested his hand over hers. Healers together they gently rested their hands on the open wound, became one when they felt the fawn's heartbeat, the flow of its blood against their skin. The pulse of their own blood echoed each other's as well as the deer's, and all three hearts beat in perfect rhythm. In that moment, though they were strangers, Magnus and Esmé shared their souls and knew one another completely. That's also when they realized that long ago The Voice had become their own, calling them to one another, to the fawn, and to this moment.

"My hands are small and I can sew very tiny stitches," she murmured, unwilling to break the bond that held them—all three—together. "I take care of many small animals, so I am not afraid. But the burns and the wound are so grievous—"

"First we need leaf poultices of yarrow to staunch the bleeding." He had already started a small fire as he unloaded herbs and bottles and leaves from his sack, packing the snow up around the sides so it would not spread, though he could not see how the larger fire had spread, for there was no wind; the air was so still he could hear every ragged breath of the tortured fawn. Magnus heated the yarrow leaves over the coals, doing what he knew to be practical, though he feared he could not save the animal. It was so tiny, and pale from loss of blood and the pain from the burns.

Something kept him from expressing his doubts. *It would no' be the hope and resolution in the wee lassie's eyes, would it now, Magnus the empty-headed fool?* If she believed they could do it, perhaps they could.

She leaned toward him at that instant and murmured, "I know we can save him—or her—whichever it be. I know it in my soul."

He fell into her silver-grey eyes, feeling their pull—and her faith and their strength. She held him captive, refusing to look away until he nodded.

That rattled him. *Magnus the Practical, that's me. I've no time for absurdities such as people reading my thoughts. Even if tis a bonny lass with long blonde hair and a heart-shaped face. I don't like it and I don't need it.* All the while this was happening, he continued making the poultice by adding heated water to the yarrow leaves.

He turned to the girl, telling her to quickly lay it directly on the open wound and cup her hand around it. She did so without question, replacing it with another when he was ready. The blood became sluggish and finally clotted. "We will need more yarrow later when the fever comes, though these leaves have helped clean the wound, so the fever may no' be as great. But we will have to wait and see.

"What now?" Esmé, who had thought herself adept at healing, realized she knew little compared to Magnus, who was as useful as he was compelling.

"I have concocted something that will help even more," he assured her.

She believed him.

"Tis a tincture of St. John's Wort. I'll get it, now the little one sleeps."

She was grateful for that, and acutely aware of the celestial buck standing behind them.

Magnus drew his precious jar from his sack, surprised to see that, miraculously, it had not been broken. "I infused fresh flowers in oil to get this beautiful and powerful red oil," he explained. He drew out some small cloths he had doubled. "Here, will you apply it?" He wiggled his long fingers. "I'm afraid I would hurt it unnecessarily."

Esmé took one of the cloths, let him pour on some oil, and turned to the fawn.

"Put it first on the open wound. It will make it numb and clean it both, and also keep it from swelling."

The fawn woke, sighing in pain.

"I am here, little one, right here." Esmé began to hum

in rhythm with her deft fingers.

As long as she kept the fawn's head in her lap, it was quiet.

"Now for the stitches." Magnus spoke so low she barely heard him. He brought out a thread she had never seen before. "It's catgut, " he said, answering her unasked question. "Sturdier than thread, and natural to a body."

And then he did the strangest thing: he dragged the needle and thread through the deep red oil from the St. John's Wort. "More caution to make sure it won't become putrid."

Nodding, she smiled. How wise he was. Especially with this weak little deer. Taking a deep breath, she held the sides of the wound together, as she had on many a rabbit or vole or fox, and began to sew gently but firmly. She kicked her recorder toward Magnus with a raised eyebrow, but at first he was too fascinated with her dexterity to look anywhere else.

They had given the fawn a draught to put it back to sleep again, and asleep it stayed. Magnus stared open-mouthed at the precise stitches Esmé took as she carefully closed the wound. They were so small they held the sides together evenly—and were, themselves, straight besides.

Not until the third time she kicked him did he pick up the recorder in his large hands. His father had given all three boys lessons, desiring that they be cultured as well as strong. Like Magnus, his father was ready for a new kind of world, or he had been long ago when his wife still lived. But Graeme and Hugh were not. They wanted to be soldiers, heroes, fighting for clan and home. Playing the recorder was not part of their plan. Nor Diarmid's. Not anymore.

Magnus had tried, but his brothers had stayed around to mock him and his big hands, so he had given up. He picked up Esmé's instrument and idly blew a note or two. Then two more. She looked up from her work and smiled at

him, and that was all it took. He found his lessons came
back to him, at least enough for him to play quietly. He
watched the fawn's heart beat through its wounded chest—
through stitches and red oil and puckered burned skin. He
saw that the heart beat slowed as he played, and though he
could not feel what the small animal felt the way he now
understood Esmé could, he could at least see the difference.

He could see, as she continued to sew, and stroke the
fawn's head and hold its feet in her palm, that she had
given herself over heart and soul to the wounded animal.

When she finished sewing, he gave her drops of the red
oil on her fingers and showed her by motioning in the air,
how she should drop it onto the burns without rubbing.
"We'll have to wait till tis somewhat more healed for that,"
he said.

She met his gaze and both realized they would stay as
long as necessary to be certain the fawn would heal fully.
They smiled at each other and did not mind.

When Esmé had finished treating the burns on the
animal's side and back, she once again followed Magnus's
instructions and lightly bound the wound with more
medicine, to keep it clean, and the burns to keep the oil in
place. Finally, she gently lifted the fawn into her lap and
took the warm medallion from her pocket. It was cool now,
but still gleaming—infused with magical light. She placed
it on top of the bandages as a final offering, a final gift of
healing from the long ago past. Then she began to play her
recorder, soothing all within its melody.

It came upon her and Magnus that they were bone-
weary from their journey.

They closed their eyes, for all they could do now was
wait.

That was when the white celestial deer finally lay
down nearby and began to speak. For a long moment, they
were awestruck by this spiritual figure. Both knew long ago
deities had taken the shape of the sacred deer.

*Only now that he sleeps can I take the time to tell ye why he has been calling ye to him for so long.*

"It's a male," Magnus said in surprise, for he had thought it a female. But Esmé only smiled a secret smile.

*Yes. The first—and only—white celestial deer born through these two centuries, for that is how the ancient gods proclaimed it. We are the protectors, the fertile, the honorable the loyal. Because the line had gone unbroken for thousands of years, the seasons change as the months pass: summer into autumn, autumn into winter, winter into spring and spring into summer. But from the moment of my son's birth, he has been in danger.*

*People have mostly forgotten the old ways, the ancient gods, the magic of sun and moon and stars. And because their belief is weak, so are we, who represent the oldest of the old, born of the Druids and before the Druids, of Celt and Roman and the Kingdom of Dalriada. There is also darkness in this world, which seeks to defeat the light. It has sought my son since birth, determined to destroy him, but an old woman came to us and let him choose two humans to help when he was most desperate. He could only speak inside their heads and not appear before them. He chose you, and I see that he chose wisely.*

*Last night the darkness came and set the blaze all round us, and I was powerless to fight it, for my son was surrounded by dark fire, and the forces of light cannot fight such a threat. Then we heard your voices coming, and even that was powerful enough to douse many of the flames. And then we saw you, and more fire consumed itself. And then you offered your tender hands—the greatest gift of all. For if he dies, our line will cease to be once I am gone. We are given one chance to procreate, and one chance only. That is why I ask you to save him.*

*I do not know yet if my son will live, but I know tis because of this danger that winter lingers oe'rlong.*

*Touch him,* the deer instructed them. It would not have

occurred to them to disobey.

Magnus moved as close to Esmé as he could and they leaned over the sleeping fawn, with her long blond hair for a curtain shutting them off from all but each other. Magnus rested his hand on top of hers upon the fawn—too young, yet, to be called a buck—and at once they had one vision and one sight. It spun with designs of Druid and Celt, with the gods on the walls and left free in the air. Century spun back upon century, belief upon belief, odd clothing upon jewelry of gold and copper. The history of the men and women who wore those clothes and that jewelry spun its story and then they moved on, and culture upon culture spun through their sight. The Old Ones, the sacrificed, the Celts and their gods, which Esmé recognized and shared into Magnus's open mind, and then century upon century, folktale upon truth upon herb upon Sight, upon healing upon war, upon death upon learning. It spun and it spun through darkness and light, and then, finally, everything grew still.

Magnus and Esmé gasped as if their bodies had actually travelled so far and so fast. But by the time they caught their breath, the fawn was still sleeping, as if there had been no disturbance at all. The two healers sat unmoving, wondering at all they had seen and felt and known in those brief flashes, from ancient times to the present. In the space of a few moments, miraculously, they had been allowed to understand for themselves the importance to the whole of Scotland of saving this tiny fawn.

Without him, the winter would never release its grip. It would become eternal.

# Chapter 15

Several times in the next few days, Esmé cleaned the wound and treated the burns, then applied fresh dressings, according to Magnus's instructions. The fawn slept on as long as Esmé sang or played the recorder.

Meanwhile, Magnus set up a crude camp, using his last flannel blanket as a kind of half-tent. He built a larger fire in the center of the fire-swept ring; it was the only place nearby where the snow was not thick and too cold to rest on. Besides, he and Esmé needed to stay close to the fawn and keep him warm. Esmé wrapped the injured animal in her plaid, which seemed to give him comfort, though she could tell he was floating somewhere away from them, because of the draughts to keep him sleeping and the fever that began to burn through his body.

Eventually, both Magnus and Esmé fell asleep, and when they woke, there was fresh prey to cook, and their damaged clothes had been replaced with sturdy new ones. Neither had spoken their concerns out loud, but they had wondered how they would survive in the cold, without food.

On that first new morning, after they ate, they began to talk.

She nestled next to him, grateful for his warmth and his wisdom and his kindness. "Ye don't believe, do ye?"

"In what?" he asked idly, concentrating on keeping his hand in his lap rather than running it through her soft gleaming hair.

"That he'll..." she swallowed dryly, "that he'll survive."

That took his attention away from her hair. Looking away, he rumbled, "Ye believe enough for both of us."

She was silent for so long that he thought she might be angry. Just when he was searching frantically for something to say, she raised her head and looked him in the eye. "I'm not sure that *is* enough. I think, no I'm certain, that believing is part of the cure."

She held his gaze, awaiting his response, but he could not think what to tell her.

"And what of the Celestial Deer? Do ye believe in him? Do ye believe that if the fawn should—" She broke off, unable to say the words.

Magnus drew her closer and felt her trembling. "Tis just…it doesn't make sense."

Esmé could not help herself; she began to giggle. "And the dream? Does that make sense? The one who haunted us and called us here, now? Waking in this snow world when we never traveled so far or so high? The crone along the way? The white buck who fades in and out of our sight? Does even one small part of it make sense?"

Shaking his head, Magnus wondered, not for the first time, if he was following in the footsteps of his ancestor, Magnus the Mad. "No, none of it. Not one tiny crumb."

She elbowed him gently in the side. "But look ye, here we are."

"Here we are," he echoed with a flicker of hope. Oh, how he wanted to believe in the enchantment that had brought him to the moment when he sat here talking magic with this amazing woman. How could he deny it, after all? She was right; all those bewitching things had happened. But he was too afraid to speak of them out loud. Afraid to admit what he felt for Esmé.

"Can ye at least believe that?"

"Aye, well, it'd be foolish to argue. But why are ye so passionate about this? Why is it so important to ye that I believe?"

Esmé drew back, struck by the question. "I just…" she hesitated, afraid to express what neither had even alluded to. "I thought, when we touched his beating heart...I felt I knew ye, that I'd always known ye. As if...as if we were brought here for some reason other than the healing." There. It was done. She could not believe she had said it out loud. If he laughed at her, or looked puzzled or blank, it would break her heart. *But I won't give up*, she thought. *Not anymore.*

Astonished by her courage—and his own cowardice— Magnus raised her chin with his finger. "Yes, I felt it too. But I was too afraid to say so. I'm an eejit; I've always been an eejit. And too big. Everyone says I'm too big. I'm a healer who can't even do his own stitches because of my clumsy large fingers. And ye are so tiny and fragile. I fear I would break ye, if no' with my body, then with my small doubts. I'd no' normally speak like this, so openly. I can no' believe I'm doing it now, but these are extraordinary circumstances. I think...it seems to me..." he stumbled over his words, "that mayhap we have known each other for a long, long time. And it frightens beyond battles or death or dishonor."

"Fear is no' the same as disbelief, Magnus." Esmé's voice shook just a little.

Just then the fawn whimpered and they turned as one to their work, to the task that had brought them together.

Esmé had been giving the animal sips of water and broth whenever it awoke. Now the fever was at its peak and the fawn shuddered and shivered. Magnus brought her handfuls of snow which she melted on a cloth and then smoothed over its body, trying to cool the fever. She was busy constantly, wetting the cloth, caressing the fawn with it, taking more melted snow from Magnus, who also saw to the broth he had made from the rabbit they'd eaten the first day.

"Isn't it time for the yarrow?" she asked him. She herself was drenched in sweat; it ran into her eyes and down her chest, and her trews were soaked.

"I'm sorry, lass, but ye have to let the fever run its course to some extent, or the poisons stay locked inside. I'll let ye know when tis time.

It seemed like days she had been battling the fever, refusing to give in, and then she heard Magnus rustling among his herbs and smelled heated yarrow leaves. She closed her eyes, leaned her head back and sighed with relief. Because she believed in Magnus.

He came to her with the poultice, but she refused to take it. Instead she guided his hands to the fawn's forehead, placed the poultice across two of his fingers and steered them to lay the leaves there gently. Magnus used his little finger to smooth the leaves down and then sat back, triumphant.

"I would never have risked it without ye." He reached for Esmé and nuzzled her neck.

She turned fully toward him. "Twas no' a risk, Magnus. Twas a gift."

They gazed at one another for a brief moment that lasted years, then moved closer until their lips were a breath apart. "Ye have saved me," he whispered.

"And ye me," she replied.

Their lips met tenderly, and he tasted her sweet, sweet kiss. He knew without asking that this was her first: full of innocence and passion, need and the gift of her heart.

# Chapter 16

For the next several hours, both hovered over the fawn, alternating tisanes of pennyroyal and yarrow leaves and trying to make the fawn more comfortable with the cool cloth. Esmé was delighted the first time she prepared the leaves properly, just as she was the first time Magnus managed to blot the cloth over the animal's body.

They smiled at each other constantly, and Magnus could not help but wonder if Esmé was right, and the believing helped, because at last the fawn began to sweat, which meant the fever was breaking. Magnus gave it some water from Esmé's small cup, and she fed it broth, a little at a time.

Esmé opened the dressing to see that the swelling had gone down and the stitches were now completely visible. And when she met the white fawn's eyes, they were clear—no longer delirious—and she swore she could see gratitude in the silvery depths.

It was still in pain, so Magnus prepared the leaves of All-heal and Esmé placed them on the wound and burns. The fawn went back to sleep.

"The Voice is gone," she said sadly, as they ate their own broth.

Magnus put his arm around her and felt her sorrow through her clothes. "Why is that, do ye think, my love?"

It was the first time he had used the word love and it sent warmth furrowing through her body. She leaned into him, into the heat and the welcome of his body. "I think tis no' necessary anymore—for us to communicate, I mean. I think its soul must rest with its body so it can fully heal, and that the voice took a great deal of energy and spirit."

*Tis odd*, Magnus thought, *that she can be so practical*

*and useful and precise, and yet so fanciful.* But he did not speak the words, because she would only point out that the voice had spoken to him as well and brought him here, and because of that, he had met Esmé. There was no getting around that one. It was, indeed, a miracle. "Aye, no doubt you're right." To punctuate his point, he kissed her.

Esmé climbed up in his lap, and curled against him, threw her arms around his neck and kissed him back with every bit of her passion and belief.

The gesture took his breath away; no woman had ever made him feel like this before. Fingers of fire raced through his veins, and he wanted her with a desire so intense it blurred his senses. He wanted her this instant—all of her— but that would have to wait.

Clinging to his greatcoat, Esmé shivered at the sensations rushing through her. She had never imagined sensations like these, even in her dreams, when she awoke hungry and aching. This ache was more than pleasant; it was ravenous and greedy, and she felt her whole world lay within it, waiting to be born.

"Do ye love your family very much?" Magnus asked at what she thought a most inappropriate time. But he knew better.

She glared at him in silence, tried to kiss him again, but, reluctantly, he drew his lips away. "I'm waiting."

"Do ye really want to know?" she asked in exasperation. "Now?"

"I most sincerely want to know. Right now."

"But why?" She wanted nothing more than to kiss for a while longer and then fall asleep in his arms.

"Ye said ye believe in me," he pointed out.

She nodded, again reluctantly.

"And when ye asked me your questions, I answered them at once, though I was afraid of your response. Is that no' so?"

"Aye," she said. She could hardly disagree.

"Weel then, please answer mine. Tis only fair."

Esmé got out of his lap, because she surely could not talk of everyday matters while she was there; it was against her desire, her will, and her common sense. "All right then." But she did not give up entirely—not while she continued to breathe. She took the leather thong from the bottom of her braid and began to unwind her long blond hair. She knew without being told that Magnus loved her hair.

"Aye, I love my family dearly. They're the best people I know, except for Breda the Brat—" she added automatically. Then she remembered all the help her sister had given her to get Esmé out of the house and on her journey. "No, even Breda the Brat. I must remember to stop calling her that."

She explained about Breda, and then it was only natural to tell him why she had needed Breda's assistance, and that led to the story of Ewan and her father and the bear, and then she had to stop to take a drink of water.

Magnus was fascinated that the amazing woman snuggled beside him had been hidden away in her home for years until The Voice called her away. Yet she had come. Had never considered staying at home where she was safe. She was more remarkable than he'd imagined.

Now that she was talking about her family, Esmé had forgotten all about kissing—for the moment. She went on to describe her much beloved Grandmother Caelia, and her great-grandmother Clare, and her grandfather Rory and her father Connall Fraser and her young brother Geordie.

"But what about your mother?" he asked, puzzled by her absence in the fascinating narrative.

Esmé had long since finished unbraiding her hair. She concentrated for a long moment on combing it out. Finally she took a deep breath. "My mother is named Sorcha MacGregor." She continued to comb; her hair was very long. "She comes and goes, rather like my other great-grandmother, Lila. She cannot seem to stay in one place for very long. So I'm very glad she brought Da home and married him. If she had no' done that, I can't imagine where we all would be. But she did, and we're together, and safe, and can choose what we want, and we're happy. Tis why I wear the Rose plaid and no' the Fraser. We all like it best, and we can no' have a hundred clans running through the house. Think how confusing it would be. And that's my home, Magnus. That's what I love—and who. Except for ye."

It was not what Magnus had thought he wanted to hear, but when she was finished, it took him only an instant to make his decision.

~ * ~

The next time they turned to their patient, he was struggling to stand.

# Chapter 17

The fawn was finally walking without difficulty. He followed both Magnus and Esmé around as they did their daily chores; he submitted meekly to their ministrations, though he began to have a kick in his step and confidence that encouraged him to hold his head high. The better he felt, the more he withdrew from them until, at last, he was as regal as his father and did not seem to remember who these two people were.

Esmé wept a little as she saw this happening day-by-day. She could not deny the emotional connection she felt with the tiny fawn who had needed them so much. In caring for him, she had woven a fine but tensile bond between them, which, like an invisible web, wound around Magnus as well. The three had shared an experience like no other that had come before, or would ever come again.

She could not dismiss so easily the empathy she'd felt for the small wounded animal. It had grown into tenderness, then fondness, then deep affection as the animal healed and grew stronger, became more himself.

Even Magnus mourned the loss of their companion. This was an exceptional creature, after all, finely honed and beautiful: no other deer came close. "But tis no' only that," he told Esmé. "When I help heal something, I give it part of myself, and in return, I receive a part of him. I never knew that before, in all my years of treating the sick and the injured. Tis a silent pact between us, a bond, ye might say." He smiled and his face shone with wonder at the revelation.

Esmé kissed his cheek tenderly. "Aye, that's it exactly." She had known that for a long time, as she used her remedies on her small menagerie at home. But it had never occurred to her as she helped treat her brother's fever. She had given Ewan something of herself, and in return, she had received something of him. He'd been in her heart, always, just as the amazing white fawn would be.

She settled against Magnus's chest, and he closed his arms around her. "Tell me, *mo-charaid*, do ye disbelieve any less?" she asked.

"Tis difficult to disbelieve when coming brought me ye. When I saw these wonders with my own eyes and felt them with my body. I'd have to call myself Magnus the Moron if I didn't come to believe just a little."

Esmé kissed his neck. "You're no' a moron. You're brilliant and caring. And handsome." She whispered this last, but he heard it just the same.

He leaned down to look into her eyes, brushing her lips with his as he did so. "Weel then, Esmé, do ye think I'd be presentable enough to meet your family? Do ye think they'd be willing to take me in?"

She sat up straight, affronted. "Take ye in as what?"

Smiling, he caressed a lock of her hair. "Why as your husband, of course. What else could I possibly mean?"

Speechless, she stared at him, stricken mute.

He took advantage of the moment by kissing her again, this time more ardently.

Throwing her arms around his neck, she returned heat for heat and passion for passion. "Yes," she said breathlessly, when she could draw away for the instant it took to release the word.

"Weel then," he replied, drowning in his need for her, "well then, we'd best be getting home. Soon!"

His betrothed could only nod vigorously.

~ * ~

That evening clouds gathered, not as if for a storm, but as if for a display. When the sun began to set, many colors streaked across the sky: fuchsias and lilacs, purples and oranges, reds and golds, swirling one into the other, then spreading across the crystalline sky. The colors and patterns held Esmé and Magnus spellbound, they were so powerful and full of beauty—a pageant laid out before them, so they could take the beauty in and hold it forever in their hearts and in their memories. Just before the golden sun touched the shimmering, snowbound earth, the white fawn leapt up before it, front legs extended in a graceful profile, and then it disappeared.

Both knew without speaking that they would never see it again.

Magnus turned to Esmé to see the colors of the sunset had reached out and curled around her, touching her everywhere in vivid hues, and outside the colors a curl of crystalline snow began at her feet and rose in a swirl of delicate ice gems about her body and her head. It was one final gift from the gods of old, and he would never forget it as long as he lived.

They fell asleep soon afterward, seduced by the lullaby of her recorder, and the stillness of the night, and the gentle breeze that sang to them as it drifted past their heads.

When they awakened in the morning, they were under a great hawthorn tree on the road south from Beauly, and everywhere the snow was melting, revealing new spring wildflowers.

Magnus and Esmé smiled at one another knowingly, but said not a word to anyone. Delighted, even by the extra mud, they headed toward home.

# Chapter 18

Breda sat by the window in the front sitting room, trying to sew stitches as fine as her sister's. She knew it was pointless, but was attempting to make a good impression on Grandmam Caelia and her father. Now that Esmé was gone, she wanted to prove she was no longer simply a brat, that she had grown worthy of their respect. The problem was, she was terrible at sewing and the expressions that crossed her face were downright comical as she struggled with thread and hoop and fabric. "I think I can get it," she whispered to her young brother more than once, "if I can just hold my mouth right." She said it, not because she believed it, but because it always made little Geordie laugh.

"Da and Grandda Rory don't think Esmé's ever coming back," Breda whispered behind her hand to the lad, as if it were a tremendously important secret, which also made him laugh. "But Grandmam Caelia and I know better. Ye mark my words, young lad."

Geordie, playing on the Brussels carpet with a wooden train, disgraced himself by giggling outright.

Pensively taking a deep breath, Breda stared longingly out the window. She'd been astonished by how much she missed her older sister. Breda had always considered Esmé an enemy—or at the very least, a bother, because she was constantly underfoot. She didn't do anything or go anywhere, so she wasn't the slightest bit interesting. But once she was gone, Breda found she missed Esmé's recorder playing in the evenings. The younger girl had always sat back and pretended not to care—had told herself she didn't. She had not realized until lately that she'd been lying to herself.

She had felt safe and comfortable knowing Esmé was always nearby and ready to help, that she grew the most delicious carrots and cabbage and onions in her garden, that she knew how to treat a scrape or a sprain or an upset stomach. And only after she was gone, had Breda come to treasure the lovely shawl her sister had embroidered for her birthday. Breda wore it all the time now, often pausing to admire the pattern of blooming roses beside a burn at either end. She did so in that moment and therefore missed the movement far beyond the window.

Geordie stood up and peered out. "Breda," he said in an odd voice.

She rose and followed his gaze, then hurried to the window, staring with her mouth open. She forgot she was holding a needle in her hand and pricked her finger deeply. She dropped the embroidery on the sofa and headed for the door, then went back for Geordie, who still stood motionless. She grabbed his hand and tugged until he followed her from the room.

"Da! Grandmam! Grandda! Come quick!"

Covering one ear with his hand to try to protect himself from her mighty voice, Geordie followed helplessly behind.

"Ye must all come at once. Esmé is home! Hurry!"

"I don't know why ye must shout so," Geordie protested.

Breda released his hand and he headed for the main door, except he was frustrated, because he couldn't see out.

The rest of the family came tumbling down the stairs, or so it seemed to Geordie, bouncing on their happiness at Breda's news.

"Are ye sure?" Da asked.

"Positive," Breda replied, "though she looks a fright."

"Is she all right?" Caelia demanded. "Is she ill?"

"How would I be knowing that, when I've only seen her from far away? But—" the girl drew out the pause until everyone was staring at her curiously. When their expressions began to turn angry, she hastened to add, "She's brought a man. He looks as much a fright as she."

The family fell silent. No one knew what to say. The three males—including Geordie—tightened their muscles as if ready to swing, and set their jaws, ready to turn the stranger away.

The two females smiled at one another, but quickly forced their lips into a long thin line.

Thus the battle lines were drawn.

They all stood where they were, as if their feet were stuck in plaster, until the door knocker rose and fell. As if released by some magic hand, everyone flew about, flustered, excited, bewildered.

Finally Geordie went to answer the door. He tried to block the threshold, but his legs weren't long enough. He glared up at wild-haired Magnus. "I'm Geordie. I'm her brother, and if I were big enough—"

"Tis happy I am to meet ye, Geordie. I'm Magnus MacLeod. And I'll tell ye a secret. I've always been too big, and tis no fun at all." He offered his hand, half-covered in dirt, the sleeve of his shirt caked with mud, but Geordie declined to take it.

"If ye hurt my sister, I'll never forgive ye."

"I never did hurt dearest Esmé; ye can ask her yourself." Magnus raised his voice slightly. "I'll swear on anything ye like she's in the same condition and health she was when she left ye. Except, mayhap, a mite more dirty."

Everyone burst into laughter at that, even Esmé, though Magnus was not certain exactly why.

"Come in, come in. Welcome home, Esmé, lassie. We've missed ye so," Da said, taking his wee girl in his arms.

Then it was Rory's turn and Breda's, and Esmé introduced Magnus each time.

Finally she turned to her Grandmother Caelia. "Esmé,

my love, tell me you're staying."

The young woman reached for Magnus's hand. "I want to, but only if ye have room and an open heart for my betrothed, who's soon to be my husband."

"Aye," Caelia said. "I knew he was coming, ye see." She swept her hand behind her to the wall above the great fireplace in the hall.

There hung a painting of Esmé surrounded by lilacs and fuchsias, purples and oranges, reds and golds, that had reached out and curled around her, touching her everywhere in vivid hues, and outside the colors a curl of crystalline snow began at her feet and rose in a swirl of delicate ice gems about her body and her head. Just visible in the background was a tall man with long dark hair, and eyes full of wonder, admiration and love.

Magnus held his betrothed's hand tightly, unable to take in a breath.

"My grandmother painted that with her pastels."

He shook his head back and forth, back and forth.

"I told ye," Esmé said. "Now do ye believe me?"

"Yes," he said simply. "How can I not?"

He reached for her and drew her into his arms, where she felt at home and on fire—both at once. She raised her face and he lowered his until his lips touched hers, softly, tenderly, with all the love and desire he had been born to give. And she, in turn gave him her heart and soul and her yielding, pliant lips, promising the world, and beguiling him with the magic that bound them from that moment to forever.

# About Kathryn Lynn Davis

Kathryn Lynn Davis was born with what the ancient Celts called "the fatal gift of the imagination: a crown of stars and a stinging sword." She had no choice but to become a writer. Since Scotland is the home of her heart, and she loves history (having a Masters in the subject), it was inevitable that she should write historical novels, most of which are set in Scotland. An award winning, New York Times best-seller, she has published eight historical novels and one historical novella.

Kathryn has a BA in English and history from the University of California, Riverside, where she graduated Magna Cum Laude, Phi Beta Kappa. She also received her MA in history there.

Toward the end of the 20th century, she gave up writing out of frustration. Only when she discovered Indie publishing did she return to her love of writing with great enthusiasm. She has re-published part of her backlist as e-books: *Child of Awe*, and the Too Deep For Tears Trilogy: *Too Deep for Tears, All We Hold Dear,* and *Somewhere Lies the Moon*. In November, 2014, she had the honor of being included in the first volume of *The Scrolls of Cridhe, Highland Winds*. That novella, *A Tear for Memory* is a prequel to her Too Deep Trilogy.

Currently, she is re-working and republishing her backlist novel, *Sing To Me Of Dreams*. She's so excited by all this activity, and all the new friends--both authors and readers--that she's made on Facebook.

Follow Kathryn on Facebook:

https://www.facebook.com/kathrynlynndavis.

# More books by Kathryn Lynn Davis

## Too Deep for Tears

Late 1800s: Three sisters. Three corners of the British Empire. Three lives intertwined... forever.

As he travels the British Empire, diplomat Charles Kittridge leaves behind three daughters: Ailsa in the Scottish Highlands; Li-an in Peking, China; and Genevra in Delhi, India. Bound by threads they neither see nor understand, the three sisters are haunted by their absent father--each in her own way. Creative and intuitive, often lost and without hope, they come together through their dreams in times of fear and need. Those dreams grow vivid, changing as these extraordinary women learn the lessons the Empire has to teach. And the all-important lessons within their own hearts. No matter the courage and passion, betrayal and loss they experience, their dreams never leave them.

In the end, they believe Charles Kittridge has the power to heal them. But the truth is far more complicated than any of them understand.

## All We Hold Dear

Book II in the Too Deep for Tears Trilogy. Full of suspense and haunting emotion, it follows Mairi, Ailsa and Alanna—three generations of Highland women--who must call on all their strength and the wisdom of the ancient Celtic gods, when strangers come to Glen Affric. The intruders bring greed, conflict and treachery, pitting brother against brother, father against son, husband against wife. Yet among them is a new love for Alanna. More mysteriously, and without intention, they reignite Ailsa's old and precious memories... In the epic struggle of man against man, and man against nature, who will suffer and who will thrive?

## Somewhere Lies the Moon

Four generations of Scottish Highland women live in Glen Affric. Their stories intersect through Ena Rose—barely past childhood, not yet a woman—who faces choices she cannot understand, and a love that may never fulfill her dreams. Ailsa Rose is content in her familiar home, until she finally recognizes the turmoil she has refused to see, the pain she knows not how to heal. She calls out across the world to her half sisters: Wan Lian, struggling to outlive the shadows of her past in a small country town in France; and Genevra, back in India, searching for her future among the multi-colored patterns engraved in her soul. Together again in their Glen Affric sanctuary, they learn that they are strong enough to face any challenge...as long as they hold on to one another.

## Child of Awe

From the moment of her birth, Muriella Calder is heiress to a great fortune many Highland clans desire to make their own. Touched by The Sight, she struggles to understand herself, while fighting those who threaten her world: the violent clans who relish war; her cunning guardian, Archibald Campbell, the powerful Earl of Argyll—callously ambitious, and bound by loyalty to the Crown; John Campbell, the Earl's second son—a strong, experienced warrior on the battlefield—who cannot begin to understand the mysterious woman he is forced to wed; and Elizabeth Campbell Maclean, a gentle woman whose heart is forfeit in a treaty with a man her father hates.

## A Tear for Memory

How can a seer paint 'Truth' when she's lived a life of lies? Will she allow a man who has twice deceived her to open her heart to the truth?

In the Highlands of Glen Affric, years after The Forty-Five—the Jacobite rising led by Bonnie Prince Charlie—Celia Rose lives happily in Faeries' Haven, where the lies that protect her from the past keep the magic and the faeries away. She finds her only magic when she paints, and "sees" things she cannot possibly know.

When a stranger comes on a mysterious errand, he threatens those who want to keep her safe at home. Little by little, he shows her new colors, new worlds and, most compelling—new passions. But he also brings danger, for he, too, lives a lie and is not what he seems. Still, danger comes in many forms, and the truth he offers leaves Celia with a difficult choice: to believe in those who loved and raised her; or trust this man, and learn the dark secret that could both destroy her innocence and forge in her a woman's heart.

## Sing to Me of Dreams

*One woman's journey of discovery...through all the mysteries of the human heart.*

As a child, Saylah held the magic and wisdom of her Salish Indian people. But when tragedy ravages the Salish, she must leave them for the world of the Ivys – an English/Scottish family whose traditions are as strange to her as her spirit world is to them. The Ivys have come to fertile British Columbia in search of paradise, but the secrets and mysteries surrounding them are overwhelming – until Saylah comes to help them understand the darkness holding them back.

Frustrated Julian Ivy, in whom sophistication and fury entwine, is drawn to Saylah's healing strength and disquieting beauty. Through sorrow and elation, the two discover the fullness of love...but no one can resolve for her the contradictions of her birthright. Following the songs of her heritage, she will finally make the most wrenching choice of all....

# Other Titles by Duncurra

## Lily Baldwin

### Jack: A Scottish Outlaw

*Freedom is not won...it is stolen*

Jack MacVie and his brother are thieves, robbing English nobles on the road north into Scotland. They're about to attack the Redesdale carriage when another band of villains, after more than Lady Redesdale's coin, sweeps down and steals their prize. Despite his hatred for the English, Jack's conscience forces him to kidnap the lady to save her life.

In the aftermath of the Berwick massacre, Lady Isabella Redesdale's world is shattered. Her mother is dead, her father lost to grief, and she's risking it all, journeying north into war-torn Scotland to be with her sister.

Although they come from different worlds, Jack and Isabella are more alike than they first realize. They both crave freedom from war and despair, but in a world where kings reign and birth dictates one's station, freedom is not won, it is stolen.

### Quinn: A Scottish Outlaw

*He is an outlaw...And the only man she can trust.*

Quinn MacVie is in pursuit of a prize, but it is unlike any plunder he has stolen before. He seeks neither gold nor jewels, but something infinitely more valuable—Lady Catarina Ravensworth. Sent by the lady's sister, who fears Catarina is in danger, Quinn's mission is to steal the lady away from Ravensworth castle. But nothing there is as Quinn expected.

Lady Catarina has been accused of a horrific crime and is forced to run or face a fate worse than death.

But she is not alone.

Thief and Scottish rebel, Quinn MacVie, is at her side. With a price on her head, they must disappear into the wilds of the Scottish Highlands where the only thing greater than the danger following at their heels is the desire burning in their hearts.

# Stephanie Joyce Cole

## Compass North

*Can you ever run away from your own life?*

Reeling from the shock of a suddenly shattered marriage, Meredith flees as far from her home in Florida as she can get without a passport: to Alaska.

After a freak accident leaves her presumed dead, she stumbles into a new identity and a new life in a quirky small town. Her friendship with a fiery and temperamental artist and her growing worry for her elderly, cranky landlady pull at the fabric of her carefully guarded secret. When a romance with a local fisherman unexpectedly blossoms, Meredith struggles to find a way to meld her past and present so that she can move into the future she craves. But someone is looking for her, someone who will threaten Meredith's dream of a reinvented life.

# Ceci Giltenan

## The Pocket Watch

*When Maggie Mitchell, is transported to the thirteenth century Highlands will Laird Logan Carr help mend her broken heart or put it in more danger than before?*

Generous, kind, and loving, Maggie nearly always puts the needs of others first. So when a mysterious elderly woman gives her an extraordinary pocket watch, telling her it's a conduit to the past, Maggie agrees to give the watch a try, if only to disprove the woman's delusion.

But it works.

Maggie finds herself in the thirteenth century Scottish Highlands, with a handsome warrior who clearly despises her. Her tender soul is caught between her own desire and the disaster she could cause for others. Will she find a way to resolve the trouble and return home within the allotted sixty days? Or will someone worthy earn her heart forever?

## The Midwife: The Pocket Watch Chronicles

*Can a twenty-first century independent woman find her true destiny, in thirteenth century Scotland?*

At his father's bidding, Cade MacKenzie begs a favor from Laird Macrae—Lady MacKenzie desperately needs the renowned Macrae midwife. Laird Macrae has no intention of sending his clan's best, instead he passes off Elsie, a young woman with little experience, as the midwife they seek.

But fate—in the form of a mysterious older woman and an extraordinary pocket watch—steps in.
Elizabeth Quinn, a disillusioned obstetrician, is transported to the thirteenth century. She switched souls with Elsie as the old woman said she would but other things don't go

quite as expected. Perhaps most unexpected was falling in love.

## Once Found: The Pocket Watch Chronicles

*Elsie thought she had found love.*

The handsome young minstrel awoke her desire and his music fed her soul. But just as love was blossoming, the inconceivable happened—Elsie awoke more than seven hundred years in the future, in someone else's body.

Gabriel Soldani thought he had found love several times, only to have it slip from his grasp. In medical school he had fallen hard for Elizabeth Quinn but their careers led them in different directions. When their paths cross again, he hopes they've been given another chance.

There's only one problem...the woman he's never forgotten doesn't remember him.

*Once love is found...and then lost...can it be found again?*

## Highland Revenge

A 35,000 word novella, originally published in the collection, Highland Winds, The Scrolls of Cridhe Volume one.

*Does he hate her clan enough to visit his vengeance on her? Or will he listen to her secret and his own heart's yearning?*

Hatred lives and breathes between medieval clans who often don't remember why feuds began in the shadowed past.

*But Eoin MacKay remembers.*

He will never forget how he was treated by Bhaltair MacNicol—the acting head of Clan MacNicol. He was lucky to escape alive, and vows to have revenge.

Years later, as laird of Clan MacKay, he gets his chance when he captures Lady Fiona MacNicol. His desire for revenge is strong but he is beguiled by his captive.

Can he forget his stubborn hatred long enough to listen to the secret she has kept for so long? And once he knows the truth, can he show her she is not alone and forsaken? In the end, is he strong enough to fight the combined hostilities and age-old grudges that demand he give her up?

## Highland Echoes

*Love echoes.*

Grace Breive is strong and independent because she has to be. She has a wee daughter to care for and, having lost her parents and husband, has no one else on whom she can rely. Driven from the only home she has ever known, she travels to Castle Sutherland to find a grandmother she never knew she had.

As Laird Sutherland's heir, Bram Sutherland understands his obligation to enter into a political marriage for the good of the clan, but he is captivated by the beautiful and resilient young mother.

Will Bram and Grace follow the dictates of their hearts, or will echoes from the past force them apart?

# Highland Angels

*Anna MacKay fears the MacLeods. Andrew MacLeod fears love.*

Anna, angry with her brother, took a walk to cool her temper. She had no intention of venturing so close to MacLeod territory—until she saw a wee lad fall through the ice.

Andrew becomes enraged when it appears the MacKay lass has abducted his son, his last precious connection to the wife he lost—until he learns the truth. Anna, risked her life to save his beloved child.

Now there is a chance to end the generations old hate and fear between their clans.

*Fate connects them. The desire for peace binds them. Will a rival tear them apart?*

# Highland Solution

*Laird Niall MacIan needs Lady Katherine Ruthven's dowry to relieve his clan's crushing debt but he has no intention of giving her his heart in the bargain.*

Niall MacIan, a Highland laird, desperately needs funds to save his impoverished clan. Lady Katherine Ruthven, a lowland heiress, is rumored to be "unmarriageable" and her uncle hopes to be granted her title and lands when the king sends her to a convent.

King David II anxious to strengthen his alliances sees a solution that will give Ruthven the title he wants, and MacIan the money he needs. Laird MacIan will receive Lady Katherine's hand along with her substantial dowry and her uncle will receive her lands and title.

Lady Katherine must forfeit everything in exchange for a

husband who does not want to be married and believes all women to be self-centered and deceitful. Can the lovely and gentle Katherine mend his heart and build a life with him or will he allow the treachery of others to destroy them?

## Highland Courage

*Her parents want a betrothal, but Mairead MacKenzie can't get married without revealing her secret and no man will wed her once he knows.*

Plain in comparison to her siblings and extremely reserved, Mairead has been called "MacKenzie's Mouse" since she was a child. No one knows the reason for her timidity and she would just as soon keep it that way. When her parents arrange a betrothal to Laird Tadhg Matheson she is horrified. She only sees one way to prevent an old secret from becoming a new scandal.

Tadhg Matheson admires and respects the MacKenzies. While an alliance with them through marriage to Mairead would be in his clan's best interest, he knows Laird MacKenzie seeks a closer alliance with another clan. When Tadhg learns of her terrible shyness and her youngest brother's fears about her, Tadhg offers for her anyway.

Secrets always have a way of revealing themselves. With Tadhg's unconditional love, can Mairead find the strength and courage she needs to handle the consequences when they do?

## Highland Intrigue

Lady Gillian MacLennan's clan needs a leader, but the last person on earth she wants as their laird is Fingal Maclan. She can neither forgive nor forget that his mother killed her father, and, by doing so, created Clan MacLennan's current desperate circumstances.

King David knows a weak clan, without a laird, can change quickly from a simple annoyance to a dangerous liability, and he cannot ignore the turmoil. The MacIan's owe him a great debt, so when he makes Fingal MacIan laird of clan MacLennan and requires that he marry Lady Gillian, Fingal is in no position to refuse.

In spite of the challenge, Fingal is confident he can rebuild her clan, ease her heartache and win her affection. However, just as love awakens, the power struggle takes a deadly turn. Can he protect her from the unknown long enough to uncover the plot against them? Or will all be lost, destroying the happiness they seek in each other's arms?

# MJ Platt

## Somewhere Montana

*Can Callum "Mac" Maclain make Sage Burnett believe in his love for her and save her from her stalker?*

Escaping from a stalker, Sage Burnett crashes her plane on a mountain, part of the ranch owned by the man who rejected her eight years ago. She still loves him and prays he isn't around because she dreads facing him to only have him reject her again.

Callum "Mac" MacLain, the ranch owner, a Marine home on medical leave rescues her from the mountain. He persuades her to stay until she heals. He realizes he is still in love with her. Can he save her from her stalker and convince her his love is real?

**Look for exciting new titles from Duncurra in 2016!**

63851750R00080

Made in the USA
Charleston, SC
15 November 2016